USA Today & Wall Street Journal Bestselling Author

The Midlife Birthday Club

A Novel

by Rachel Hanna

To my reader,

I want to tell you something I've never really told anyone before.

In 2019, I was forty-six years old. I had a husband I adored, kids I was proud of, a house I loved, and, on paper, my life looked like one that had worked out. By every measure that gets posted on a Christmas card, I was fine.

And quietly, where nobody could see, I was losing hope.

I had been writing books since 2012. Seven years of trying to make this author thing work, and I felt like the world had forgotten me. That's the exact phrase I used. I know because I made a video about it. Not for the internet. Not for an audience. Just for me, talking into my phone because I needed to say the thing out loud and didn't have anywhere else to put it. I said I felt washed up. I said I wasn't even fifty yet, and I already felt like I'd missed my window. I didn't know what to do next.

And then I wrote *The Beach House*.

I didn't know when I started it that it would be the book that changed everything. I just wrote a story about a woman whose life cracked open in a way she didn't ask for, and who had to decide what came next. I wrote her because I needed her. And when that book went out into the world, something I had stopped believing was possible happened. You found me. Readers found me. Women who had been quietly carrying their own version of "I think the world forgot me" picked up that book and wrote to tell me they felt seen. I had a tribe. I had been writing for them all along, and I just hadn't known their faces yet.

I'm fifty-three now. Seven years on the other side of that video.

I wrote *The Midlife Birthday Club* because the women in this story are sitting in the same chair I was sitting in then. Claire is invisible inside her own marriage. Harper has built a career so high she can't see anything else from up there. Nina is buried in a grief that just won't move. And instead of letting fifty happen to them quietly, the way birthdays seem to happen to women our age, they make a pact. One scary or uncomfortable thing every month for a year.

What I learned writing this book is what I wish someone had told me at forty-six. The version of yourself you think you've lost is still in there. She's just waiting for you to do something brave enough to wake her up.

Like all my books, this one is a clean read. Just kisses, no spice. But these women carry real things, and I tried hard not to flinch when they did. You'll find pieces of yourself in all three of them, I think, the way I did.

Thank you for being here. Whether this is your first Rachel Hanna book or your fiftieth, I'm so glad you opened it.

Happy reading! Rachel Hanna

Claire had changed the napkin color at least four times, and that number was probably a bit lower than the actual count. It was best not to count, or else she might think she was losing what little was left of her mind.

The first choice was coral, because it looked elegant in Pinterest photos, but it arrived looking like raw salmon. Definitely not a sophisticated salmon, more like a cafeteria salmon. The kind served on a Styrofoam plate with a little piece of parsley that had given up on life.

The kind you'd find at a hospital just before being admitted for food poisoning, a few hours after eating it.

The kind she would imagine someone would eat

in prison. Wait? Did they get salmon in prison? Unlikely.

She had returned those napkins and then ordered sage green, a color she often loved. But Greg said it made the table look like a hospital. It was the most he had said to her in three days, so at least that was a win. His vocal cords had apparently not locked up after all.

Her third choice was ivory, but ivory napkins on a white tablecloth looked dirty, and Claire Morrison was not going to have a dirty table. She was turning fifty. This was an important time, and the table needed to rise to the occasion.

She finally settled on dusty rose. Nobody would notice or even comment on them, which pretty much summed up the last decade of her life. These were the kinds of things that mattered only to Claire. Sadly, the most important thing she would give herself on this monumental birthday was dusty rose napkins. Yay.

The house smelled of the mouth-watering rosemary chicken she had made and the lemon pound cake she had been baking since noon, because she knew Nina's favorite bakery on Bay Street had closed eight months earlier.

Nobody made pound cake the way they did, except for Claire, who had called the bakery's former owner to ask for the recipe. They told her it was a family secret, and she spent three weekends reverse-engineering it from memory and using a YouTube tutorial, but she did not need to tell anyone about that part.

She had not told Nina she was even baking the cake, just in case it didn't turn out well. But Nina needed something to make her smile, and Claire hoped this would do it.

The guest bathroom had been cleaned twice because once simply wasn't enough. The fancy soap shaped like a magnolia blossom sat in its little dish, smelling like someone's rich grandmother. She wished she were the rich grandmother. Or a grandmother at all.

The truth was, even though she had two grown children, she hardly saw them these days. Her son Adam lived in Germany with his new wife, and her daughter Molly lived in California. They were chasing life, like she once did, but she wished they were closer and stayed in touch more.

Three bottles of wine sat on the kitchen counter because Claire was not sure whether this was a two- or a three-bottle night. With her friends, it was often a three-bottle night.

Turning fifty with your two best friends while your husband sat in the next room, acting as if you had personally offended him by simply continuing to exist on the planet, seemed like it could go either way.

Greg was sitting in the den.

Greg was *always* sitting in the den.

If Claire died tomorrow, the paramedics would find Greg sitting in the den, watching something on his laptop with his earbuds in, the recliner engaged, completely unaware that his wife had ceased to be alive in the next room. He might notice by dinner-time if there was no food on the table. *Maybe*.

He had wished her happy birthday that morning in the same way that he confirmed dentist appoint-ments. He acknowledged it, noted it, and then moved on. One more thing checked off his list. *Root canal, check! Wife turns fifty, check!*

Twenty-six years of marriage, and the man had given her a gift card. And it wasn't even a specific gift card, like the ones you'd give to someone you actually knew. Nope, it was one of those universal cards that you could use in any store, whether it was the dollar store or the department store.

It seemed choosing an actual retailer would require more thought about her than he was willing to invest in her fiftieth year on earth.

How exciting that she could now go to the grocery store and buy toilet paper with her brand-new, shiny gift card. Wasn't she the luckiest woman in town?

She had smiled and thanked him, of course, and then put it in the junk drawer next to the scissors that no longer cut anything and the batteries that were probably dead.

She positioned the dahlia stem in the Mason jar that she had wrapped with twine because she saw it on Pinterest and thought it looked charming. It did look charming.

Everything Claire touched looked charming.

She had a gift for that, making things beautiful for others as she slowly disappeared. For Claire, life felt like a big hole in the floor, swallowing her up bit by bit while no one noticed. Or cared.

"You know," Greg said from the doorway. She was so startled by his rare presence in the kitchen during baseball hours that it felt like she was looking at wildlife. "You could just take them out to dinner. Keep it simple."

Claire put another dahlia stem into the Mason jar and counted to three in her mind. She had learned years earlier that the first thing she wanted to say to her husband was probably not the best.

The first thing in this case would have been: *When was the last time you made anything simple for me? Don't you like to make life harder for me?*

Or maybe she would've said, *Hey, gift card guy, why don't you just shut your mouth and go away?*

But what she said was, "I like doing this. It's important to me."

He shrugged, the universal gesture of a man who had made his suggestion and considered his job done.

"I'll be in the den. The Braves are on at seven. They're replaying the '95 World Series again. It never gets old."

He said it with more enthusiasm than he had shown at the party, at her birthday, or at Claire's new dress, which was still hanging on the back of the bedroom door with the tags on it because she had not decided whether it made her look like she was trying too hard for a party she was having in her own house.

She listened to his footsteps go down the hall, followed by the loud, familiar thump as he fell into the recliner. It was then followed by the opening bars of a pregame commentary, which sounded like the worst thing on earth to Claire. Men just sitting there giving their opinions on other men hitting balls through the air… for hours on end. No thanks.

These were the sounds of her marriage, predictable as a metronome and twice as monotonous. How had it gotten this bad?

Of course, other marriages were way worse. This was something she told herself regularly. Greg could be a cheater. He wasn't. Greg could be abusive. He wasn't. He just didn't seem to notice she was alive anymore.

Claire looked down at her hands. She had flour under her fingernails. She looked at her thin gold wedding band. She had not taken it off in twenty-six years. It just sat there, a remnant of the romance she once felt, a fleeting moment in time.

Who are you?

The thought arrived sharp and uninvited as it always did, like a car alarm going off at 3:00 in the morning.

But she shook it off because she had a party to finish. Claire Morrison did one thing very well - made others feel valued and seen. Boy, she wished someone would do that for her.

Harper arrived at 5:47, thirteen minutes early, because Harper Ellis had never been late for anything in her life. She had even been born early, and she honestly hadn't been late a day since.

She came through the front door without knocking, as she usually did. She had never knocked at

Claire's house, not once in all the years they'd known each other. Claire had stopped locking the front door on days when she knew Harper was expected because Harper once stood on the porch for forty-five seconds and decided that was an unreasonable waiting time and then called to ask if Claire was dead.

Spoiler alert: Claire answered the phone, and she wasn't dead.

She was wearing a silk blouse the color of emeralds, wide-legged black trousers, and heels that qualified as an architectural achievement. There was no way Claire could ever have worn those. She would have toppled over immediately.

Harper's blond hair was blown out to a shine that suggested either a very fancy salon or forces beyond mortal understanding. She held two bottles of champagne, a gift bag from a store Claire could not even afford to walk past, and the energy of a woman who had gone to back-to-back meetings since seven that morning and had just decided to be fabulous anyway.

That was Harper. Always fabulous, never a hair out of place. She was the epitome of "never let them see you sweat."

"Claire Morrison, if you tell me that you baked a three-layer cake from scratch for your own birthday, I swear I will sit on your front porch and weep."

"It's just simple pound cake, and it's for all of us." Claire knew that was a lie. Nothing she ever did was simple.

"I brought cheese from that place on King Street. The one with the goat out front."

"The goat's name is Gerald."

"Of course, you know the goat's name."

Harper set the champagne on the counter and pulled Claire into a hug. She smelled like Chanel.

She held on a moment too long, and Claire felt it. Harper never held on longer than necessary.

Then Harper pulled back and looked at her with those sharp green eyes. She never missed anything, not in their thirty years of friendship.

"You look beautiful. How are you? Don't you dare say fine."

Claire opened her mouth, then closed it. She smiled the smile she had perfected for parent-teacher conferences and dinner parties. Broad enough to look natural, but small enough not to look psychotic.

"I'm so glad you're here."

Harper looked at her for a second. Claire could almost see the gears turning behind her eyes. The same analytical mind that ran a $200 million division, deciding whether or not she was going to push further or let it go.

She let it go. For now.

"Where's Greg?"

"Nineteen ninety-five."

"The Braves?"

"The Braves."

Harper poured herself a glass of water and then leaned against the counter, her arms crossed.

For just a moment, Claire imagined them when they were twenty years old again, standing in their dorm at the College of Charleston, eating ramen and planning lives that had not happened yet.

It made Claire's chest ache.

They'd all had such big plans. Big dreams. They would live together in a fancy apartment in NYC. Or maybe they would rent a villa in Italy and meet Italian men whose sole jobs would be to feed them pasta and grapes.

Greg had never once fed her grapes.

"She's coming, right?" Harper asked.

They both knew who *she* was.

"She said she was."

"You know that's not the same thing as actually showing up."

"I know."

They looked at each other, and the worry they

shared about Nina Vargas passed between them, as it had for the last eighteen months now.

Nina showed up at 6:22, which was a little late for the old Nina but practically a miracle for the Nina who had existed since her beloved David died. They gave her grace. She'd been through one of the worst things a spouse could go through.

Claire heard the car in the driveway first. There was a long pause. She and Harper both noticed it. The *pause*.

Nina did that a lot now. She got to where she was going, then stayed in the car for a while, as if she had to gather the pieces of herself before she could walk into a room and pretend they were all in the right place. As if she were a jigsaw puzzle scattered across the floor of her car, and it took her a while to pick up as many pieces as she could to be whole. There were always a few missing pieces.

Claire opened the front door and watched Nina come up the walkway. She was thinner than the last time Claire had seen her. It was not terribly alarming, but she did notice that her collarbones looked different from what they had been before.

She wore a soft gray cable-knit sweater. Claire

immediately recognized it as one of David's. He had bought it in Charleston on their tenth anniversary at that shop on Market Street that sold overpriced cashmere to tourists. David had always had good taste.

Nina wore it the way you wear a hug from someone who is no longer there to give one. It was obvious she was trying to physically wrap herself in the memory of her beloved husband.

She held a bottle of wine in one hand and a small potted succulent, wrapped in brown paper, in the other.

"Here, it's a housewarming gift," Nina said blankly, holding up the plant. "I know you've lived here for decades, but I haven't been over in a while, so." A small smile flickered across her face, like a fleeting ghost of a joke. Nina used to be so funny, but in the kind of way a person doesn't even realize they're funny. That was gone now. Claire hadn't seen that side of her in almost two years now.

Claire wanted to wrap her in a blanket and not let her go for six months. Instead, she took the succulent.

"I love it. Come on in. Harper's already halfway through the cheese board."

"I am not!" Harper called from the kitchen. "All I've had are two crackers."

"And a quarter pound of brie," Claire said, pointing to the quickly emptying board.

"Well, brie doesn't count. Brie is like a condiment."

Nina's mouth twitched, but it still was not quite a smile. It was the place where a smile would go if she had one to give. She stepped inside.

"It smells so good in here. I haven't cooked a real meal in a couple of weeks. Poor Lucia has been living off frozen waffles."

"Well, she's sixteen," Harper said, handing Nina a glass of wine. "That's a balanced diet for her age."

"Waffles?"

"Yep."

They all moved into the dining room, and Claire watched Nina take in the table, the dusty rose napkins, the Mason jars of flowers, and the three place settings on the good china that only came out for Thanksgiving and birthdays, or the occasional Tuesday when Claire just needed to feel like her life had some kind of ceremony.

"This is beautiful, Claire," Nina said. "You really did a great job putting this together."

Greg appeared in the doorway. Claire felt the familiar tension he brought. Him and his khakis and his College of Charleston T-shirt, with his earbuds draped around his neck. They were not even the good earbuds. They were from an older time, but he said they worked better than the newer ones. Greg was a man lost in the mid-nineties.

He stood in the doorway like a man who intended to be there only briefly. He wasn't planning to hang around and celebrate with his wife and her two best friends. He had things to do, a wife to ignore.

"Ladies, happy birthday. Y'all need anything?"

"We're fine, Greg," Claire said, her jaw tightening.

"Holler if you do."

He gave a little wave and then retreated back to 1995.

Claire felt Harper's eyes on her like a laser beam, but she chose not to look.

They sat down, and Claire brought out the chicken, roasted vegetables, and the rolls she had made from her mother's recipe. No one could beat those yeast rolls.

Harper opened the champagne, and Nina held her glass up.

"To fifty."

They clinked and drank.

For a while, it was good. Just the three of them, the way it used to be.

Harper telling a story about a man in her office who sent a company-wide email meant for his girlfriend, and the forty-five minutes of chaos that followed.

Nina laughing at Harper's impression of the man's face when he realized what he had done.

Claire refilling glasses, passing the bread, and, for the first time in weeks, feeling like she existed.

They talked about Lucia, who was apparently going through a phase in which she communicated exclusively through eye rolls and sighs.

They talked about Harper's assistant, James, who had started bringing his emotional support ferret to the office.

They talked about the bookstore on Bay Street that was closing and whether the new coffee shop on Edisto was any good.

They talked about the woman at Claire's school who had shown up for the faculty meeting with her shirt inside out and had not noticed until lunch.

But they did *not* talk about Greg.

And they did *not* talk about David.

And they did *not* talk about the fact that Harper ate dinner alone most nights or that Nina's house on Edisto was so quiet she had started leaving the television on just to hear another human voice.

Those things sat at the table with them, taking up space like uninvited guests.

It was Nina who finally said his name.

They were on the second bottle of wine. Claire had brought out the pound cake, and Nina had taken one bite before going very still.

"This tastes like Barton's," she said softly.

"Does it?" Claire kept her voice light and casual, as if she hadn't spent hours making sure that cake was right.

"Claire, you called Susie to ask for the recipe?"

"She wouldn't give it to me. Family secret or some such nonsense."

"What did you do?"

"I might have spent three weekends recreating it from memory. I don't know if I can pay my light bill this month because I spent all the money on flour."

Nina stared at her and then looked down at the cake. She pressed her fingers to her mouth and laughed. But then the laugh turned into something else, something wet and raw.

"David used to bring me a slice every Friday. He'd stop on his way home from the office and get one slice, not the whole cake, just the one slice because he said that was the perfect amount, and it made it more special." She wiped her eyes with the back of her hand. "I'm sorry. I'm sorry. Y'all, I didn't mean to."

"Don't you dare apologize," Harper said. Her

voice was tender and fierce at the same time in a way that only Harper could accomplish.

"He was a good man," Claire said. "He deserves to be talked about."

It was true, and it needed to be said out loud.

"He was the best." Nina picked up her fork and took another bite. "Man, he would have loved this. He would have eaten three slices and blamed it on the dog. And you know he would have been right here in the middle of this birthday party, even if we had said it was a ladies' night."

"You don't have a dog," Harper said, obviously not getting the point at all.

"That never stopped him."

They laughed, all three of them. The kind of laughter that has tears hiding behind it.

Outside, the Beaufort evening was doing what Beaufort evenings do, turning the sky pink and gold over the river and sending crickets onstage for their nightly performance.

Claire had lived here for twenty-four years, and she still had never tired of it. Some nights, the beauty of the place made her ache. The same way a song could remind you of someone you missed.

"Should we move to the porch?" Claire asked.

Harper grabbed the wine, and Nina took the cake. Claire grabbed three forks, because she knew these women well enough to know that nobody was going to bother with plates. They would share that cake as they'd done in college.

They settled into the chairs on Claire's screened porch, the marsh stretching out dark beyond the yard. The air was thick with salt and pluff mud, and the last heat of the day was finally letting go. Somewhere out on the water, she could hear a boat engine humming. Closer, a frog was making its opinions known.

For a few minutes, none of them spoke.

They just sat there, these three women turning fifty years old, drinking wine, listening to the Lowcountry breathe.

"Can I say something?" Claire finally asked.

The funny thing was, her voice sounded strange to her own ears. She hadn't meant to speak at all.

"Always," Nina said.

Claire looked out at the marsh.

"I spent four solid hours getting ready for tonight. I changed the color of those napkins four times. I baked a cake from a recipe that doesn't exist so that it would taste like a bakery that closed months ago." She paused a moment. "And the most exciting thing Greg said to me today was that the Braves game started at seven."

Harper was quiet. So was Nina.

The frog was not quiet, but the frog really was not part of the conversation.

"I'm fifty years old," Claire said, "and I don't know who I am without a to-do list."

That part she had not meant to say. She had meant to say something funny or light, something wrapped up in a joke.

But the wine, the cake, David's name hanging in the air, and those stupid dusty-rose napkins that nobody had even noticed cracked open a door she had been trying to keep shut.

Harper reached over and took her hand. She didn't say anything. She just held it.

"I can't feel anything," Nina blurted out.

They both looked at her.

She was staring straight ahead with her wine glass resting on her knee, and David's sweater pulled tight around her.

"I know that I'm supposed to be getting better, you know, getting over it. Elena keeps saying I need to get out more. Lucia looks at me like she's been waiting for me to come back from wherever I went. And I want to get back. I just don't know how. It's like there's this glass wall between me and everything and everybody, and I keep pushing against it, but I can't get through."

"I had dinner alone four nights last week," Harper

said quietly. "On the fifth night, I went to a restaurant and had dinner alone so it would feel different, but it did not. It felt just as lonely as eating over my kitchen sink."

Nobody laughed.

Nobody tried to fix it.

They just all sat there, three women on a porch in Beaufort, South Carolina, finally laying it all out there.

Claire looked at her friends.

Harper, who could command a boardroom but could not fill a dinner table.

Nina, who had lost the love of her life and just wanted to remember how to feel, how to want.

And then there was herself, fifty years old, four napkin colors deep, and wondering where the woman she used to be had gone.

Where had she gone?

Where had all those hopes and dreams she had had as a college student wandered off to?

"Well," Claire said, "happy birthday to us."

Nina snorted. Harper chuckled.

And the night kept going the way all Lowcountry nights do, slow and warm.

CHAPTER 2

Harper Ellis had *not* planned to tell the truth tonight.

Telling the truth at a birthday party was just a big downer. Birthday parties were for cake, dancing, and laughter. Nobody wanted the truth for their birthday.

She had planned to show up, drink champagne, eat Claire's impossibly good food, and then perform that version of herself that she had been performing for thirty years.

The sharp, funny, put-together professional.

The woman who had it all figured out.

The woman who did not need anyone, not really, because needing people was a vulnerability, and vulnerability was a liability.

Harper Ellis did not carry liabilities on her balance sheet.

But Claire had said, "I don't know who I am without a to-do list."

And Nina had said, "I can't feel anything."

And then, seemingly without her permission, she had heard her own voice say that thing about eating dinner alone five nights in a row. Truth be told, she almost always ate dinner alone. Five days wasn't her longest stretch.

Now all three of them were sitting on the dark porch with their defenses down like houses that had lost their walls during a hurricane. And Harper had no idea how to put hers back up.

She also did not feel like she wanted to, and that was an even more alarming realization.

Apparently, the wine was doing its job.

The second bottle was almost gone, and Harper was considering a third, which she didn't normally do on a weeknight.

But turning fifty while confessing your extreme loneliness to your two best friends on a screened porch in Beaufort felt like maybe it was an exception.

"Now I want to say something," Harper said. "And I need you both to not make this into some big deal."

"Okay, well, that's a promising start," Claire said, rolling her eyes.

"I'm serious."

"So am I. Every time somebody says, 'Oh, don't make this a big deal,' it always feels like a very big deal. But please, proceed."

Harper sucked in a breath. The salty marsh air sat on her tongue. She had never loved the Lowcountry the way that Claire and Nina did. Charleston was a city to her, a place with great restaurants and good business, and a condo with a view she rarely even looked at.

But on nights like this, on Claire's porch with frogs making noise and the water somewhere beyond the dark, she could almost see why people wrote poems about this place. Although at night, she found it spooky.

"So Jordan called me."

The porch went even more silent. She was pretty sure the frog paused and had his little hand cupped over his ear.

"When?" Claire asked.

"Three weeks ago."

"Three weeks?" Nina turned in her chair. "You sat on this information for *three whole weeks?*"

"I didn't sit on it. I just handled it."

"And what does 'handled it' mean?" Claire asked.

"I told him I was busy and I hung up."

"Harper!"

"What? I was busy. I had a quarterly review."

"You always have a quarterly review," Claire said, taking a sip of her wine.

"Quarterly means four times a year, Claire. I mean, it's just math."

Nina made a sound that almost sounded like a laugh, but Harper couldn't tell in the dark.

Nina leaned back in her chair. "What did he want?"

"I don't know. I didn't stay on the phone long enough to find out."

"So you panicked." Claire didn't say it as a question. She made a statement. An assumption.

"I don't panic. I prioritize. I make difficult decisions. Fast."

"You prioritized running away from the only man who ever made you happy," Claire said, a slight edge to her voice. "He loves you, Harper. And you love him, whether you want to admit it or not."

Harper opened her mouth to argue, but found that she really did not have anything to say because Claire was right, and the three of them knew it.

Jordan Beck was the only man who had ever gotten past Harper's defenses. She had punished him for that by leaving.

That was a few years ago. How had so much time gone by? Time seemed to be moving faster with each passing year.

She had not had a serious relationship since then, unless you counted the relationship with her very fancy espresso machine. Although she still didn't know how some of the buttons worked.

"He probably just wanted to talk," Claire said gently.

"People don't call their ex-girlfriends after years to talk."

"Then what do they call for?"

"I don't know. Closure, curiosity, and someone who might split the streaming password with them. Again, I don't know."

"Or maybe," Nina said, "he misses you."

Harper took an extraordinarily long sip of wine. She did not want to think about Jordan missing her.

She did not want to picture him in his workshop in Mount Pleasant, with sawdust on his jeans, that half smile he wore whenever she said something sarcastic and he chose to find it charming rather than hurtful.

Jordan built things with his hands. Bookshelves, tables, and a rocking chair he made for his mother's birthday from reclaimed wood. He was the kind of man who measured twice and cut once, in wood-working and in life.

Harper was the kind of woman who cut first, never measured, and then pretended the uneven edges were intentional.

They had been *terrible* for each other.

They had been *perfect* for each other.

Both things were true, and that was irritating.

"Can we talk about something else?" Harper begged.

"We can," Claire said, "but I do want it on the record that you brought him up, not us."

"Noted," Harper said, holding up her glass of wine and faking a toast to the air.

"And let's also note that you've been thinking about him for three weeks," Claire reiterated.

"Also noted. Moving on."

But they did not move on, really, because that was the thing about this porch and these nights with these two particular women. Moving on was what Harper did in boardrooms and conference calls. But here with Claire and Nina, conversations did not move on. They circled and settled and came back when you thought they were done with them.

"Do you remember that night that we decided to move in together?" Claire asked.

The question came out of nowhere.

"Sophomore year," Nina said. "Your dorm room. We had been studying for that awful econ final. Professor Anglin. What an awful little man he was."

"You weren't studying," Harper said. "You were eating a bag of Doritos and reading a magazine that you'd hidden inside your textbook."

"That's called multitasking."

"That's called getting a C minus."

"Hey, it was a solid C minus," Nina said, chuckling.

Claire tucked her feet underneath her in the way that she had been sitting since she was nineteen years old, maybe even before.

"We were in my room, and the power went out. Do y'all remember this? Like the whole building was completely black. We just sat there in the dark, and we talked for hours."

Harper remembered.

She remembered the three of them snuggled in on Claire's narrow dorm room bed with a flashlight propped up on a pillow.

They had talked about what they wanted their lives to look like.

Claire wanted a house with a big wraparound porch and a husband who danced with her in the kitchen.

Nina wanted to travel, cook, and have a family that ate dinner together every night.

And Harper wanted to run something. She didn't even know what it was. She just wanted to be in charge of something big and important. She wanted to be so good at it that nobody could ignore her.

In a way, they had all gotten what they wanted, all three of them.

But it had not looked at all the way they thought it would.

"You know, sometimes I think about that night and how young and sure we were of everything that was going to happen, as if we could just will it to be so." She paused. "I was going to be an artist, remember?"

"You were good," Nina said. "I mean, really, really good."

"I was fine. As I got older, I guess I got more practical. Most people can't make a living as a painter. I realized I needed to get realistic."

"You got married, Claire. That was the end of your dreams. Happens to most married people. You pick a person, and you put your dreams away," Harper said matter-of-factly.

Claire looked at her sideways, a small smile pulling at the corner of her mouth. She understood Harper's sarcastic sense of humor.

For just a moment, Harper could see the twenty-year-old Claire beneath the fifty-year-old Claire, the girl who used to stay up until two in the morning, painting in the art building and coming home smelling of turpentine.

"You know, I haven't held a paintbrush in twenty-seven years," Claire admitted. "Think about that. Twenty-seven years that I've deprived myself of doing something that I used to love."

The number hung between them like a heavy fog.

"David always said I should write a cookbook," Nina said quietly. "His grandmother's recipes, Elena's recipes, all the food that I learned to make once I was in his family. He said I should write it all down. That way Lucia would have it one day, but I never did. I just kept saying I would get to it."

"Well, you still could," Harper said. "We're not about to enter the nursing home, Nina."

"I know. I keep telling myself that, but you know, there's a difference between *could* and *will*. I've been stuck in *could* for my entire adult life."

The porch went quiet again.

The frogs had resumed their concert and seemed to have invited more frogs to their band. A breeze came off the marsh, smelling of salt and jasmine.

Harper reached into her purse.

There was no warning that she was going to do it. She did not even know herself.

Her hand found the first pen she could, her Montblanc, the one she used to sign contracts at every meeting and to move millions from one column to another in a spreadsheet.

She picked up one of Claire's dusty rose napkins from the table, the ones nobody had really noticed, the ones Claire had changed four times.

"What are you doing?" Claire asked.

"Something impulsive, which I would like to ask each of you not to hold against me later," she said, waving her finger at them. "I've had quite a bit of wine. Just remember that."

She uncapped the pen and wrote on the napkin in her sharp, slanted, professional handwriting.

The Pact.

In big, bold letters.

"Oh, good Lord," Nina said. "What kind of craziness are you concocting now?"

Harper kept writing.

"Number one. We do something every month that scares us. It can't just be an inconvenience or a mild annoyance. It has to scare us."

"Harper." Claire said her name like a warning.

"Number two. It has to be something none of us has ever done before. So if you've already done it, it doesn't count. It has to be genuinely new. And since the three of us have lived very small lives up until now, that shouldn't be too hard."

"Are you writing a *contract* on my napkin?"

"Number three. We have to do it together. All three of us. No backing out. No excuses. No, I have a headache, or I have a meeting, or I need to reorganize my pantry."

"I reorganized that pantry one time, and I'll never live it down."

"It was alphabetical, Claire."

"Well, alphabetical is a valid system."

Harper held the napkin in the air. It felt almost official, but mostly ridiculous. Again, wine was involved.

"One year," she said. "Twelve months, twelve adventures, and we take turns picking. And it has to scare all three of us. And nobody can quit."

Nina stared at the napkin as if it might bite her. "But everything scares me. I'm scared of my own mailbox. Trust me, for me, the bar is extremely low."

"Good, then you'll have plenty of options."

"What if one of us picks something that's genuinely dangerous?" Claire asked. "Like bungee jumping or swimming with sharks or eating that sushi down at the gas station on the corner?"

"Well, then we die doing something interesting for the first time in years," Harper said, shrugging.

"Okay, that's definitely not comforting."

"It's not supposed to be comforting. It's supposed to be a wake-up call. We've been stuck in our lives for years, and now we're a half a century into this thing. It's time to shake it up!"

Harper looked at her friends. Claire had her flour-dusted hands folded in her lap. Nina was wearing her dead husband's sweater, trying desperately just to feel something, anything.

And then there was herself, Harper Ellis, fifty years old, vice president of a division that generated more revenue than most companies, eating toast over the sink five nights a week because setting a table for one person felt like the ultimate defeat.

"Look, we're three intelligent, interesting, capable women," Harper said. "We're currently living as if we decided the good part of our lives is over. And I refuse to accept that. I refuse to think that fifty means we're done."

"Okay, I need a system," Claire said.

"Of course you do."

"I mean, like a rotation. I pick one month, you pick one month, Nina picks one month, and then we cycle around. Four rounds of three."

"Is it going to have to be color-coded?" Harper asked, rolling her eyes.

"Do not test me."

Nina had not said a word. She was just staring at the napkin in Harper's hand.

"You know, David would have loved this," she finally said. "He would have made such a spreadsheet, and it would have been color-coded by difficulty level. He was such a nerd."

"He was the best nerd," Claire said. "He would have signed that napkin so fast that the ink would not have even been dry."

She smiled, this time a real one. It was like a tiny little pilot light that had been out for a long time and was just flickering back to life.

"He would have told me to say yes."

"So then say yes," Harper pleaded.

Nina looked at her, then looked at Claire, looked out at the marsh for a moment, and then held out her hand.

"Give me that pen."

Harper handed it over, and Nina signed her name on the napkin beneath the rules in that looping cursive script that she'd had since college.

She passed the pen to Claire, who signed in her small, precise handwriting, the same handwriting that had shown up on decades of Christmas cards and grocery lists.

Harper signed last.

Her signature was sharp and slanted, the same one she put on contracts worth a lot of money, but it had never felt more important than it did on this dusty rose napkin on a screened porch in Beaufort at 10:30 on a Tuesday night.

"Well, it's official," Harper said.

"It's a napkin," Claire said.

"But it's a napkin with intentions."

Claire rolled her eyes. "That's not legally binding."

"Listen, Claire, I'm the one with the lawyers, okay? You let me worry about what's binding."

Nina took the napkin from Harper's hand and stared at it.

Three full signatures, three rules, and a napkin that was so thin you could see the porch light through it.

"I want to pick first," Nina said quickly.

Claire and Harper both looked at her with something close to shock because Nina had not volunteered to do anything in eighteen months.

"I thought we were doing a rotation," Claire said.

"Well, we are, but I'm rotating myself to the front."

Harper tried not to smile. "What did you have in mind?"

"Not yet. I have to think about it, but I'm going to make sure it scares all three of us."

"More or less than gas station sushi?" Claire asked.

"Oh, much more."

Nina stood up from her chair, still holding the napkin.

She looked at it one more time and then handed it to Claire.

"Put this somewhere safe."

Claire took it like it was something precious, which it was.

"I'll just put it on the fridge."

"The fridge?" Harper said. "You mean we just made a life-altering pact, and you're going to stick it under a magnet on the fridge?"

"The fridge is the most important surface in the house. Everything that matters ends up on the fridge."

"She's right," Nina said. "I mean, permission slips, report cards, that kind of thing. Drawings, wedding invitations. It all goes on the fridge."

Harper rolled her eyes. "Nothing goes on my fridge."

"The fridge it is," Claire said.

They stood on the front porch for another minute, the three of them, and Harper felt something she had not felt in so long.

Anticipation. Maybe even a little excitement.

"I should head back," Nina said. "Lucia has probably burned the house down by now."

"She's sixteen, not six," Claire said.

"Which is why I said burned, not flooded, because now she knows how to use the stove. Unfortunately, she does not always remember to turn it off."

They pulled each other into a tight group hug, something they'd done when saying goodbye since they were in college.

They walked Nina to her car. The night air was thick and warm. All the stars were out, and the crickets were giving the frogs a run for their money in the who-can-be-louder competition.

Nina got into her car and started the engine. She rolled down her window.

"Harper?"

"Yeah?"

"Call him back."

Before Harper could say anything else, Nina pulled out of the driveway and disappeared down the dark road toward Edisto Island.

And Harper just stood there in Claire's front yard

at eleven o'clock at night, watching the taillights fade and thinking about the man who built rocking chairs out of old barns.

"You okay?" Claire asked from beside her.

"I'm fine."

"Harper."

"I'm terrified."

Claire put her arm through Harper's, and they stood there, two women in a front yard, looking at the place where Nina's car used to be.

"Good," Claire said. "I think that's the whole point."

Nina woke up on the wrong side of the bed. David's side, to be exact.

She had once again rolled over there in her sleep, the way she did at least a couple of times a week, reaching for the warmth she wanted that was no longer there.

She would always wake up with her face pressed into his pillow that had long since stopped smelling like him. She had kept the pillow anyway. She had kept *everything*.

His terry cloth robe was still on the hook behind the bathroom door, even though she hated it because it was so poofy and heavy that it made the door hard to open. No matter how many times she'd complained about it, somehow it would end up there again and again.

His reading glasses were still on the nightstand, even though she hated those too. The round ones never looked great on his face, but he said he liked them.

It was funny how all the little things that made a marriage interesting, and the things you may not love about your spouse's fashion or decor choices, became so important when they were gone.

She tried not to think too hard about all the times they had fought over the pettiest of things, although they did not fight much in their marriage.

He would get a kick out of the fact that she was still annoyed by his huge bathrobe and circular glasses.

His boots were by the back door, still flecked with the marsh mud he had tracked in the last time he walked through it, a Tuesday in April, eighteen months ago.

She knew it was a Tuesday because that was the day he died, and she had memorized every detail of it, the way that you memorize the most traumatic moment of your life. Like a movie playing in your mind that you can't stop. Like a remote control that doesn't work, and you can't leave the room. You're stuck there, reliving it over and over for eternity.

She lay there for a moment, staring up at the ceiling. The fan turned in a slow, lazy circle. It needed to be dusted. She would get to it at some point. Dust was the least of her problems.

David had installed it during their first summer on Edisto because the August heat was so thick you could practically eat it with a spoon. There was nothing like Lowcountry heat.

He had gotten the wiring wrong twice before finally getting it right, and he refused to call an electrician because he was stubborn.

She had stood at the bottom of the ladder, handing him the tools and trying not to laugh every time he swore in Spanish, which his mother had taught him was the only acceptable language for profanity.

The fan worked perfectly. It had outlasted him by a year and a half, which seemed like a cruel joke that the universe specialized in lately.

She hoped she never had to replace it.

Who knew that a ceiling fan would mean so much when someone was gone?

She got up and made the bed because she always made the bed every morning.

She tucked David's side in tight the way he liked it and then smoothed the quilt Elena had given them as a wedding gift, the one with the pattern Elena's mother had brought from Oaxaca sixty years ago.

She went to the bathroom, brushed her teeth, and

looked at herself in the mirror. Now she saw a woman who was fifty years old and tired in a way that sleep just couldn't fix.

She went to the kitchen and made one cup of coffee. She used to make two cups. For months after David died, she kept making two cups out of habit.

The second one would just sit on the counter and get cold until she poured it down the sink at noon, feeling like she was pouring her husband down the sink.

Now she just made one cup.

Elena said it was progress, but Nina just called it math. Why waste money making coffee for someone who couldn't drink it anymore?

She had enjoyed her dinner with Harper and Claire the night before. And there was a part of her that was even the tiniest bit excited about their pact.

Although they did not all share the same birthday, they had decided to celebrate together because they would all be turning fifty within just a few months of each other.

The three of them had shared all of life's biggest events, good and bad, since they met in college. She realized what an extreme blessing and privilege it was to have strong women in her life who had supported her every step of the way, including the day that David had died.

They had been there in the aftermath, like two steady guards standing on either side of her, bringing food, helping to organize the funeral, talking Lucia through the loss of her dad, trying to keep Elena, David's mother, at bay in the moments when Nina just needed to be alone.

But there was only so much friends could do. Grief wasn't something you could really share with other people. It was something you had to carry alone. It was love with nowhere to go, after all. And although Harper and Claire loved David, they couldn't share in the immense grief Nina felt at losing her soulmate.

She looked out the window in the kitchen over the marsh. David had fallen in love with the view the first time the realtor had brought them here twelve years ago.

He had stood at the window with his hands in his pockets and watched an egret lift off from the grass.

"This is it. This is where we should live, Nina. Forever."

Just like that.

There was no deliberation, no weighing pros and cons. David made decisions with his whole soul. He walked into a room and knew.

He had looked at Nina across a crowded lecture

hall during their junior year at the College of Charleston, and he knew.

And he stood at this very window and knew.

Nina had loved that about him. Sometimes, she also found it maddening because she was a thinker. She needed to weigh things and turn them over in her mind fifteen times before committing.

David used to make fun of her about it.

"You're going to think yourself out of your own life, mi amor."

He had been right about that, too.

She sipped on her coffee and watched the marsh. The tide was coming in, so the water was creeping up over the mud in a slow, inevitable way, turning the flat brown landscape into something alive.

A heron stood on one leg near the dock, patient as a saint. Fiddler crabs scuttled around the waterline.

Edisto was beautiful. Nina knew it was beautiful, but right now she couldn't feel it. The only thing she ever felt was sadness, like a heavy weight around her shoulders, pulling her down ever so slowly.

That was the thing about grief that nobody explained to you. It did not just take the person. It took the ability to experience the world as you used to.

All the colors of the rainbow were dimmer. Food

tasted like nothing. Music was just background noise.

Their beloved marsh was just water, mud, and birds when it had been the most beautiful place she had ever seen.

Now it was just the place where David was not.

"Mom?"

Nina turned, a bit startled out of her memories.

Lucia was standing in the kitchen doorway, wearing an oversized Mickey Mouse T-shirt and shorts, her dark hair in the kind of knot that suggested she had slept on it wet and was not planning to fix it. Young people could get away with things like that. If she'd done it as a fifty-year-old woman, she'd look like a bridge troll.

She had David's eyes. She had his dark brown, almost black eyes with lashes so thick they looked fake. Sometimes it made Nina feel jealous. Oh, to be young again.

Every time she looked at her daughter, she saw his face, and it was both the greatest comfort and the worst pain of her life.

"Morning, baby. There's coffee."

"I don't drink coffee. I'm sixteen." Lucia stared at her like she'd lost her mind.

"Oh. Well, I was drinking coffee at fourteen."

"Grandma says you were drinking milk with a splash of coffee in it at twelve."

"Yeah, well, Grandma exaggerates."

"Grandma says that you say that every single time."

Nina rarely saw her mother these days, since her mother now lived in Washington State with her new husband, Jerry. They liked to travel the country in their motorhome, but they rarely made time to come see Nina and Lucia. Maybe it was because Nina was too much now, with all her grief and sadness. Too much of a downer, she supposed.

Lucia opened the refrigerator and stood in front of it the way all teenagers do, like staring at it long enough might cause something more desirable to materialize. Maybe a pizza or a dozen doughnuts.

She finally shut it, holding a cup of yogurt and a look of resignation, like she was going to eat it as her last meal.

"We need groceries," she said.

"I know," Nina said.

"No, like we actually *need* them. Not, 'oh, we're just low on a few things.' The freezer is literally full of ice and three frozen waffles. That's it. That's all we have."

"Okay, I'll go today."

"Well, you said that on Thursday."

Nina took a breath.

She knew Lucia was not being mean. She was just being sixteen, which meant she was being honest in the way that only somebody with no filter and lots of feelings could be.

Lucia had spent the last eighteen months watching her mom move through the house like a ghost. She was probably very tired of it, and she had every right to be. Nina was tired of it, but she still could not seem to change it.

She had one parent who wasn't there and one who was barely hanging on.

"I'll go after you leave for school," Nina said. "Make me a list."

"There's a list on the fridge. It's been there since last week."

Nina looked over at the refrigerator, and there was, in fact, a list written in Lucia's sharp handwriting, which looked nothing like David's and nothing like Nina's, and was entirely and fiercely her own.

Below the list, held by a magnet shaped like a palm tree that David had bought at a gas station because he loved collecting tacky magnets the way some people collected art, was a picture that Claire had taken and sent in the group chat three days ago.

The napkin.

The pact.

Three signatures in different handwriting.

Claire had taken a photo of it for her fridge, and Nina had seen it when it came through on her phone, lying in bed at 11:30, wearing David's sweater. She had stared at it for a long time, feeling as if she were seeing a stranger wearing her face. *Who was this woman with the dead eyes?*

She had printed it out the next morning. She did not know why. She just felt like she had to.

"What is that?" Lucia asked, following her gaze.

"It's a pact. Claire, Harper, and I made it on our birthday."

"A pact to do what?"

"One scary thing a month for a year."

Lucia stared at her, then she looked back at the napkin photo. Then she looked back at her mother. There was a look on her face that Nina could not quite place.

Maybe surprise, or hope, or the careful guardedness of a girl who had learned not to get excited about her mother's plans because her mother's plans often dissolved before they even started.

"Scary like what?"

"I don't know yet. I said I'd pick the first one, though."

"Wait, you volunteered to go first?"

"Is that so hard to believe?"

"Yeah, kinda."

It should have stung, but it did not because Lucia was right. Nina, or at least the Nina of the last eighteen months, did not volunteer for things.

She did not initiate.

She just showed up when she had to, went through the motions, then came home, sat on the couch, and watched TV until she no longer cared how late it was, before justifying going to bed.

That Nina would never have signed that napkin on a porch at 10:30 at night and told her friends she wanted to go first.

But she had.

She had signed it, and she had meant it.

She did not entirely understand why, except that when Harper held up the napkin, something in Nina's chest had shifted. It wasn't a big shift, not the kind you could see from outside.

More like a window cracking open just an inch in a room that had been sealed shut for a long time. The kind where dust coughs out between the cracks and chokes you.

"I think it's cool," Lucia said.

She said it kind of casually as she spooned out her yogurt, not looking at Nina, because teenagers deliver their most important statements without looking at their parents.

"Yeah?"

"Yeah."

A pause.

"I think Dad would think it was cool, too."

Nina's grip tightened around her coffee mug. Lucia rarely mentioned her father. When she did, it was brief, bright, and over before you could brace yourself.

"He would," Nina said. "And he'd probably want to come."

"Oh, he would definitely want to come," Lucia said, laughing.

"And then he'd be terrible at whatever it was and love every second of it."

They smiled at each other for a brief moment.

Lucia picked up her backpack. "I gotta go. The bus comes in ten minutes."

"Do you have money for lunch?"

"Mom, nobody uses cash."

"Okay, well, is your account thing loaded?"

"It's fine." She paused for a moment at the door. "Go to the grocery store. For real this time."

"I will."

"And don't sit in the parking lot for forty-five minutes before you go in."

Nina hadn't realized that Lucia knew about that.

Of course she did, though. Lucia noticed everything the same way David did.

"I'll try," Nina said.

"That's all I'm asking."

Lucia gave a small wave and then was gone, the screen door banging shut behind her.

Nina stood alone in the kitchen with her one cup of coffee, the sound of the marsh, the napkin on the fridge, and the daughter who had just asked her, in the most Lucia way possible, to please come back to life.

Elena arrived at eleven with a casserole dish and a purpose, as usual.

Nina heard the car before she saw it because Elena drove a fifteen-year-old Honda Civic that announced its presence the way a brass band might in a parade.

The engine rattled, and three mechanics had failed to fix it, but Elena refused to buy a new car because this one had been David's last car.

It was the one he had driven the day he died, and Elena would sooner walk to Beaufort barefoot than let it go. She acted as though it were a classic car that would be worth a lot of money one day.

That was very doubtful.

She came through the back door without knocking, which was exactly what Elena always did. And Nina had spent years learning to accept it.

Elena had a key. She used that key whenever she felt like it, which was very often, and she always brought some kind of food, which made it a little harder to complain.

"Mija," Elena said, setting the dish on the counter. She gave Nina a quick, practiced glance, one she had perfected over decades of mothering David. Although Nina was her daughter-in-law, as far as Elena was concerned, she was her daughter.

She checked her for weight loss, dark circles under her eyes, signs that she wasn't eating, sleeping, or doing the basic work of just remaining alive.

"You look thin."

"You always say I look thin."

"Because you are always thin. This is not a mystery." She opened the refrigerator and made a sound that was a bit of a sigh, but had a little judgment and prayer mixed in. "Nina, there's nothing in here."

"There's yogurt."

"Yogurt is not food. Yogurt is what food eats." She closed the refrigerator. "I brought mole con pollo.

You will eat it today, not tomorrow. Not a maybe. Today."

"Elena, don't—"

"I promised my son, in all my prayers, that I would take care of his family, and I cannot take care of a family that lives on yogurt and frozen waffles."

There it was.

Her son.

Elena always said it in the way she said everything about David, with a fierceness that left absolutely no room for argument. One did not argue with Elena. There was no reason to because you would never win.

Her grief was very different from Nina's.

Nina's grief was a fog, gray and suffocating, muffling everything around her. It was a monster that stole every good thing.

Elena's grief was a bonfire, loud, visible, and consuming. She carried it not as a burden, but as a badge of honor, as proof that she had loved someone so big and survived losing him, and she intended to honor him every single day until God took her too.

Nina sometimes envied Elena's grief. At least Elena could feel hers. She could feel emotions. She still had a purpose, even if that purpose was driving Nina crazy.

Elena was moving through the kitchen now,

wiping down counters that did not need wiping, rearranging things that did not need rearranging, her small hands always busy because Elena's hands could never be still.

She was barely five feet tall, but she filled every room she entered. David had gotten his warmth and stubbornness from her.

"I heard about the birthday," Elena said.

"It was nice. Claire cooked. We had cake. It was great."

"And?"

"And what?"

"Lucia told me about the napkin."

Well, of course she did.

Lucia and Elena had a gossip pipeline that operated entirely outside of Nina's knowledge or consent. They texted in Spanish, which Nina understood about 60%, and the other 40% was almost certainly about her.

"It's just something fun," Nina said. "Claire, Harper, and I are going to try new things. One time a month."

Elena stopped wiping the counter. She turned and looked at Nina. The face Elena was trying not to make was the most obvious. She was trying not to cry, not to hope, and not to say the wrong thing, all at the same time.

"Good," Elena said.

Just that one word.

"Elena, don't make this a big thing."

"I'm not making it a big thing."

She picked up her purse, set it down, and picked it up again. "I'm just saying that my son would be so glad to know that his wife is choosing to live. David would be so pleased. That's all I'm saying."

She kissed Nina's cheek, smelling like cold cream, garlic, and that Jean Naté body splash that she'd been wearing since 1987, at least according to David.

She was out the back door before Nina could respond, her Honda rattling down the driveway like a one-car noisy parade.

Nina stood there in the kitchen again. The casserole still sat on the counter, warm. The napkin photo still hung on the fridge.

And through the window, the marsh was fully flooded now, the water catching the late morning sun, and a pelican diving for fish.

David used to watch the pelicans for hours. He said they were proof that you did not have to be graceful to be effective.

"Would you look at that," he would say, pointing at a pelican crashing into the water beak-first.

"Absolutely no style at all, but gets that fish every darn time."

Nina watched the pelican surface with a fish in its pouch, triumphant and ridiculous, and she felt something.

It was small. It was so small she almost missed it. Just a flicker, like a muscle she had forgotten even existed.

It wasn't joy. It wasn't happiness. It was the precursor to those things. The ingredients.

She picked up her phone and opened the group chat. Claire had sent a photo that morning of the napkin on her fridge, slightly crooked.

Harper had replied with a single emoji, a pair of eyes, which was Harper's version of enthusiasm.

Nina typed:

> I know what the first adventure is.

Three dots from Claire immediately.
Then Harper:

> If it's bungee jumping, I'm invoking a
> veto I just invented.

Nina typed:

> Karaoke.

A long pause.

Then Claire:

Oh no.

Harper:

Absolutely not.

Nina:

You said no backing out. Rule three. It's on the napkin.

Harper:

I will buy that napkin from you. Name your price. I have access to millions, and I am not above insider trading, if necessary.

Claire:

She's right. We signed it. Where are we going?

Nina thought about it for a moment.

She wanted to go somewhere where none of them would be recognized, far enough from Charleston, Beaufort, and Edisto that Harper wouldn't worry about running into a colleague, and Claire wouldn't worry about running into a parent from school.

Somewhere that had cheap beer, bad lighting, and a stage that had seen worse than three fifty-year-old women butchering a Shania Twain song.

Nina:

> How about Walterboro? There's this place called Hank's. They do it on Friday nights.

Harper:

> How do you know about a karaoke bar in Walterboro?

Nina:

> Lucia told me about it once. Apparently, it's legendary.

Harper:

> Legendary for what?

Nina:

> She didn't say, and I chose not to ask any follow-up questions.

Claire:

> Dear Lord, I haven't sung in public since college. I sang at that open mic at the Windjammer, and somebody asked me to stop. Like, literally said, please stop.

Harper:

> Was it that bartender? The one with the gold tooth and the tattoo of his grandmother?

Claire:

> It was the bouncer. He was very polite about it. I guess I should be glad he didn't throw me out of the place.

Nina laughed. She was alone in her kitchen with her phone in one hand and coffee going cold on the counter, as it usually did. But she laughed. The sound of it startled her.

It was loud in the quiet house and even louder than the television she had left on. Louder than the ceiling fan David had installed. Slightly louder than the grief that had been the only voice in this kitchen for eighteen months.

She looked at Elena's dish, which was still warm, that was made with those same hands that had taught her beloved David to cook. The same hands that had held Nina at the funeral when her legs stopped working, that had been showing up at this back door every week for eighteen months with food and a love so fierce it sometimes felt like she was being hit by a very small but very determined truck over and over.

Nina uncovered the dish and grabbed a fork. She ate standing at her kitchen counter, looking at the water.

And the mole con pollo tasted like Elena's kitchen, which tasted like David's childhood, which tasted just like love.

Nina ate the whole thing.

Then she grabbed Lucia's grocery list off the fridge, picked up her keys, and drove to the store.

She only sat in her car in the parking lot for ten minutes, and that was progress.

CHAPTER 4

Claire chose to pick Nina up first because Nina was simply a flight risk.

Not literally.

Nina had said she was coming to karaoke. She had texted the group chat that morning, "I'm in, I'm coming, so please stop asking me if I'm coming."

But Claire knew Nina the way you know weather patterns after thirty years, and she could feel the hesitation under those words, the part of Nina that was already building a case for why she should just stay home.

A headache or Lucia needing her, a vague sense of not feeling up to it, which had been Nina's default setting for eighteen months now.

It was convincing enough to fool anyone who did not love her.

Nina preferred to stay home lately, but she wasn't getting out of this. That was part of the pact.

So Claire drove straight to Edisto first.

She pulled into Nina's crushed shell driveway at 5:15 and found her sitting on the front porch, wearing jeans and a black top. Her hair was down for the first time in months.

She looked like a woman who got dressed with some purpose, rather than just grabbing whatever was in her closet or something David used to wear.

It was such a small thing, hair down instead of pulled back.

Claire noticed it the way she noticed the napkins and the flower arrangements and all the details other people walked past.

Nina got in the car. "Don't you say a word about my hair."

"I wasn't going to say anything."

"But you were thinking it."

"I was thinking that you looked nice. I didn't know that was a crime."

"I know it's been a year and a half since I've gone anywhere that isn't the grocery store or Elena's house, so I figured I should make an effort."

"Well, you look beautiful."

"Stop it."

"Okay."

They drove toward Beaufort to pick up the road to Walterboro.

The late afternoon light was doing what it did in the Lowcountry, with gold pouring through the live oaks that lined the two-lane road. Spanish moss swayed in that lazy rhythm that made everything feel like it was happening at half speed.

Claire loved this drive.

She loved every part of this world, the way the landscape shifted from an island to a marsh to a mainland, yet it never lost its character. It was wild and green and warm.

Nina was quiet, just looking out the window, so Claire let her be.

One of the things she had learned about grief, or about Nina's grief specifically, was that silence was not always an emptiness. Sometimes it was just Nina being in the world without needing words.

"Lucia made me promise to take a video," Nina finally said.

"You mean of us singing?"

"Yeah. She said, and I'm quoting, 'I need proof that you actually did something fun for once.'"

"That girl is something else."

"Yeah, but she's not wrong."

Claire's phone buzzed in the cup holder, a text from Harper.

I'm already here. I've got us a table. It's way worse than I imagined. Much, much worse. This place has peanut shells on the floor.

Ten seconds later.

I'm ordering a drink, possibly several.

Nina read the text and laughed under her breath. "Of course she's already there. Harper has not been late for anything in her entire life."

"I remember one time she told us she was born two weeks early. She couldn't even wait until her due date."

"Hey, you remember when she showed up to your wedding rehearsal an hour early and ended up directing the florist?"

"I remember the florist cried," Claire said, laughing.

"The arrangements were beautiful, though."

"Yes, the arrangements were perfect. The florist quit the very next day."

They were both laughing now, that easy laughter of people who had three decades of shared stories to pull from. They never ran out of material.

Claire felt the particular magic of their long friendship, the way it could take just the smallest memory and blow it up into something warm enough to hold.

～

Hank's was pretty much as bad as Harper had promised.

It sat at the edge of Walterboro's main drag, in a building that had probably housed four or five different businesses over the years and had never been committed to any of them.

The sign was hand-painted and missing an apostrophe. The parking lot was gravel. There was a neon Budweiser sign in the window and a chalkboard sign by the door that read "Karaoke Fridays."

Inside, the place was dim and loud, and it smelled like beer and popcorn and that particular funk that a bar gets after forty years of spilled drinks on poorly cared-for wooden floors.

There were peanut shells everywhere, as Harper had warned them. Christmas lights hung from the ceiling year-round, which gave the whole room a slightly unhinged festive quality. A small stage was in the corner, complete with a microphone stand and two speakers.

The speakers looked like they had survived some

sort of war, and a screen displayed the lyrics to Sweet Caroline in bright blue font while a man in a trucker hat sang with the passion of someone auditioning for a role he was definitely not going to get.

Harper was sitting at a high-top table near the back, drinking something with a lime in it. She was wearing silk because, of course, she was. She was Harper in a bar with peanut shells on the floor, and Claire just loved her for it.

"This place is one big health code violation," Harper said instead of saying hello.

"It just has character," Claire said.

"Character is what realtors say when a house has termites."

Nina slid onto the stool next to her and looked around the room with wide eyes.

"This is absolutely incredible. I swear David would have loved this place." She said it lightly and easily.

Claire and Harper both caught it, the way David's name landed without the usual heavy gravity, and they looked at each other like, *did you hear that*? That was different. That was good.

A waitress appeared next to them. She was young, maybe twenty-five years old, with an impossibly high ponytail. "Y'all singing tonight?"

"We are," Nina said before Claire or Harper could try to get out of it.

"Well, the sign-up sheet's over there by the stage. Hank puts you in order. What can I get y'all to drink?"

Claire got a glass of white wine, which arrived in a glass that had clearly been designed for a totally different beverage. Harper was already on her second vodka soda. Nina ordered a beer, which surprised both of them because Nina had always been a wine person.

Maybe this was just a beer kind of night. Hank's kind of demanded that.

"Okay," Claire said, "we need a plan."

"It's karaoke, not a military operation," Harper said.

"Well, everything benefits from having a plan. So do we each have to sing a solo? Are we doing a group number? Do we pick our own songs, or are we going to pick songs for each other?"

"If you pick my song, I swear I will walk out of this building right now and drive back to Charleston, and neither of you will ever see me again," Harper said.

"Okay, group number it is," Nina said. "One song together. That's the pact. We do things together."

"All right, what song?" Claire asked.

They stared at each other.

The bar was filling up around them.

The man in the trucker hat had finished Sweet Caroline with modest applause and was now replaced by two women in matching denim jackets that they had apparently bedazzled.

They were attempting *Islands in the Stream* with more enthusiasm than accuracy. The Christmas lights blinked, probably because they were faulty or maybe shocked at how off-key the women were.

Peanut shells crunched all around them, and Hank, who turned out to be a large man with an even larger beard, had a surprisingly gentle voice.

"Shania Twain," Nina suddenly said.

Claire looked at her.

"Which one?"

"You know which one."

Claire did know. They all knew.

It was a song they had played on repeat in their apartment, the three of them dancing around in their tiny galley kitchen with wooden spoons as microphones. Of course, this was when they were in their early twenties and convinced they were invincible. This was well before real life had taken hold of them and showed them who was boss.

"Man! I Feel Like a Woman," Claire said.

"Absolutely not," Harper said. "That song has a dance break, and I am not planning to stand up there and do a dance break."

"Rule three," Nina said. "No backing out."

"I'm not backing out. I'm establishing boundaries. My old therapist said that was healthy."

"Harper, we sang this song at every party for two years. We sang it at Claire's bachelorette, remember? We sang it at my wedding reception after David drank too many mojitos and started doing the electric slide by himself."

"That man was a national treasure," Harper said, putting her hand on her chest.

"This is *our* song," Nina said. "It has always been our song."

Harper took a drink and then set the glass down.

She looked at Nina, then at Claire, and then at the stage with its war-torn speakers and blue-font lyric screen.

"Fine," she said, "but if anyone from my office sees this, I'm going to blame both of you and claim that I was put under duress."

Claire went to sign them up. She wrote their names on the sheet in her small, precise handwriting.

Claire, Harper, and Nina: "Man! I Feel Like a Woman"

Hank looked at the sheet, then looked at her and nodded. He understood that every person who got up there was committing an act of bravery, whether the singer knew it or not.

"You're up in four," he said. "Good luck."

"Thank you."

"Oh, you're going to need it."

"Well, that was less encouraging than I had hoped."

Hank smiled. "Everybody's terrible. That's the point."

The four performances before them passed in a blur of nerves. Claire drank her wine way too fast, then ordered another.

Harper had switched to water because she was taking this seriously, which meant she was actually terrified, because Harper only got that disciplined when she was really scared.

Nina was peeling the label off her beer bottle in long, careful strips. This was a habit she'd had since college. It was a tiny slice of the old Nina coming back to life.

This was the girl she had met thirty years ago, nervous and quiet, and doing something with her hands to keep herself from running screaming out the door.

A man sang *"Friends in Low Places"* and brought the house down.

Then a couple sang *"You're the One That I Want"* and forgot half the words.

A woman sang Patsy Cline's *"Crazy"* so beautifully that the whole bar went quiet, and Claire thought, *What is she doing in Walterboro, and why is she not on stage somewhere?*

Then she thought, *What am I doing in Walterboro?*

And then she thought, *I'm about to stand on a stage and sing Shania Twain, and I can't carry a tune in a bucket, and this was a very, very terrible idea.*

"Claire, Harper, and Nina," Hank called on the microphone. "Y'all are up."

None of them moved.

"We have to go up there now," Claire said in a loud whisper. Her legs felt like they were made of lead.

"Yes, I'm aware," Harper said, also not moving.

"That man said our names."

"I heard him."

Nina stood up. She said nothing, but she stood and began walking toward the stage.

Her back was straight. Her hands were shaking.

She didn't even look behind to see if they were following her. She just went.

Claire and Harper looked at each other.

The woman who had not felt anything for the last year and a half was walking toward the stage, doing it first, and she was going to do it alone if she had to. So they followed her.

The stage was smaller than it looked from the table, and the lights were way brighter.

The microphone was warm from the last singer's hand. Claire took one mic. Harper took another. And Nina stood between them.

For a moment, the three of them just looked out at the bar. It was very full now, at least forty people, and most of them already had drinks.

All of them stared at the stage, waiting to be entertained, but knowing they would have to accept whatever they got. That was the magic of karaoke. Nobody expected Celine Dion. They expected Bubba from the mechanic shop down the road, drunk on too much beer and a misconception of his talents.

The opening guitar riff started, and the words appeared on the screen in blue, and Claire's mind went completely blank.

But then Nina started singing.

She was awful.

Her voice was thin and slightly flat, and she was at least half a beat behind the music, but it didn't matter. It did not matter one bit because she was singing.

Nina Vargas, who had spent eighteen months standing behind a glass wall watching the world go by, the woman who couldn't feel a thing, who sat in parking lots gathering herself before she could walk into a room, was now standing on a stage in a dive bar singing Shania Twain.

Her voice cracked on the first verse, but she kept going. Claire jumped in. Her voice was better than she remembered, or maybe it was just louder, which, at Hank's, amounted to about the same thing.

She found the melody, held onto it, and leaned into Nina. She sang the words they had been singing since they were way younger, words about feeling alive and wanting to go out and wanting a night to be wild and free.

The lyrics had meant something different when she was younger. Back then, they were an anthem. At fifty, they were a prayer.

Harper was last to start singing. She stood rigid for about four bars, clutching the microphone like a life preserver. And then something shifted. Claire saw it happen in real time.

There was a loosening in Harper's shoulders, an

unclenching of her jaw. There was a moment where the woman who controlled everything decided she was in control of absolutely nothing.

Harper opened her mouth and sang loudly. She was off-key and way too loud, but she didn't care. She was performing. She was pointing at the audience. She was doing dance breaks.

Harper Ellis, vice president of a $200 million division, was doing Shania Twain's dance break in a bar with peanut shells on the floor.

And she was magnificent.

The bar was right there with them. Claire did not know when it happened, but somewhere between the first and second choruses, the room had decided these women were their people.

They were clapping. Somebody was whistling. The couple who sang You're the One That I Want were on their feet dancing.

Hank was nodding from behind the soundboard with a satisfied expression.

By the final chorus, they were shouting more than singing, arms around each other, completely out of tune and out of sync.

Claire felt something bubbling up in her body that she didn't know was there.

She felt joy. She felt stupid, reckless joy.

She had not felt this since she was young enough

to believe that dancing in the kitchen with a wooden spoon was all the purpose her life needed.

The song ended. The bar erupted in applause and cheers. It was full-throated, slightly drunk, and very genuine.

These people had just watched three women do something brave and beautiful.

Claire stood on that stage with Nina on one side and Harper on the other and thought, *I forgot about this. I forgot what it feels like to do something that has absolutely no purpose but to just feel alive.*

They walked off the stage on their shaky legs. Harper's hands were trembling. Nina's eyes were wet, and Claire could not stop smiling.

The man in the trucker hat bought them a round. The Patsy Cline woman raised her glass from across the bar, and the waitress with the ponytail said, "Well, y'all were the best kind of bad," which Claire decided must have been a compliment.

They didn't leave the bar for another two hours. They sat at their high-top table, drinking, talking, and laughing in the way only friends can after they've done something scary or crazy and actually survived it.

They replayed the performance moment by moment.

Harper's dance break.

Nina's voice cracking on the high note.

Claire forgetting the words to the bridge even though she had sung the song about four hundred times in her life.

"I forgot the words," Claire said, "to a song I've been singing for decades. How is that possible? Should I get checked by a doctor?"

"Stage fright erases everything," Nina said. "I forgot my own name up there for a minute."

"I didn't forget anything," Harper said, smiling. "I was perfect."

"You pointed at a man in the front row and winked at him. It was very cringey," Claire said.

"It felt right in the moment. That man and I will always have that," she said, playfully putting her hand over her heart.

"He blushed, Harper. A grown man blushed."

"You're welcome."

Nina had her phone out.

She had recorded a shaky ten seconds of the performance.

They could barely see anything through the poor lighting and the crowd, but she texted it to Lucia with the caption, "proof."

Lucia's response came back almost instantly. Three skull emojis, which apparently meant she was dying laughing. Nina figured it was a compliment, but she was not quite sure.

"Elena is going to see this," Nina said, looking at her phone. "Lucia will show her, and Elena will have opinions."

"Oh, Elena has opinions about everything," Claire said. "Elena once had opinions about the way I folded towels."

"Well, were you folding them wrong?" Harper asked.

"Apparently, there is a correct way to fold towels, and it has been passed down through Elena's family for generations. I was disrespecting her entire lineage by folding in thirds instead of halves."

They laughed until Claire's ribs ached.

The bar was starting to thin out, with serious karaoke performers leaving and allowing the closing-time stragglers to come in.

Hank was wiping down the soundboard with a cloth. He was humming something that sounded much like a Willie Nelson song.

"We should go," Claire said, looking at the time. It was past eleven. She had a forty-five-minute drive back to Beaufort, and she still needed to get Nina back to Edisto. Harper had an hour to Charleston on a weeknight.

They were fifty years old, out past eleven on a Friday at a karaoke bar on the outskirts of town. The absurdity made Claire want to laugh and cry.

She wanted to call her twenty-year-old self to report that the future would be confusing and not without surprises.

They walked into the parking lot. The night was cool. Claire's car sat under a street lamp that buzzed and flickered. They stood beside it but did not get in.

"Month one," Harper said. "Done." She did a little check mark with her finger in the air.

"That was the most fun I've had in years," Claire said, and she actually meant it. She meant it with her entire body, which was still buzzing from her time on the stage and maybe from the wine.

It was still buzzing from the feeling of doing something useless and joyful for absolutely no reason except that she had promised on a napkin that she would.

"So who picks next month?" Nina asked.

"Me," Harper said, "Rotation. Nina picked this one, I pick month two, Claire picks month three."

"It better be something good," Claire said.

"Remember, it has to scare us," Nina reminded.

"Oh, it will. Trust me."

Harper hugged both of them, lingering a bit longer than she normally would. She got in her car and headed toward Charleston, her taillights disappearing down the dark road.

Claire drove Nina to Edisto. The road was empty and dark, the marshes invisible on either side.

Nina was quiet in the passenger seat, but it was a different kind of quiet than Claire had gotten used to over the last year or so. It was the quiet of somebody who was thinking about what had just happened, not what they had lost.

"Claire?"

"Yeah?"

"Thank you for driving to Edisto to get me. You didn't have to do that. I know it's way out of your way."

"It's not out of the way."

"It's forty-five minutes out of the way."

"Nina."

"Yeah?"

"It's never out of the way."

Nina didn't say anything else because she didn't need to.

Claire dropped her off at the cottage on Edisto and watched her walk up the porch steps. Lucia's bedroom light was on, and Nina waved once from the door. Then Claire drove home.

It was almost one in the morning when she pulled into the driveway in Beaufort.

The house was dark.

Greg was asleep.

She walked inside as quietly as she could, hung up her keys, and stood in the kitchen staring at the napkin on the fridge.

Three signatures.

Three rules.

Month one.

Done.

Her phone buzzed. It was a text from Harper.

> For the record, I was incredible up there.

Then Nina responded.

> You pointed at a stranger and winked. It was so cringey, as my daughter would say.

Harper:

> I was commanding the room. It's called leadership skills.

Claire:

> Good night, you two.

Harper:

> Good night. Month two is going to be absolutely terrifying. You've been warned.

Nina:

> Good night. Thank you. Both of you.

Claire stood in her dark kitchen with the phone in her hand, smiling at the screen full of messages.

She had loved these women for 30 years and realized that Greg had not texted her once tonight. He had never asked where she was, if she was safe, or when she would be home.

He had gone to bed, left the porch light off, and not wondered about her at all.

She put her phone on the counter and looked at the napkin once again.

She turned off the kitchen light and walked to the bedroom where her husband of twenty-six years was sleeping on his side of the bed, facing the wall, breathing deeply.

It was the unbothered breath of a man who had not even noticed his wife had just done the bravest thing she had done in a decade.

Claire stood in the doorway for a long time.

Then she went to the guest room, took out her sketchbook from the shelf where it had been sitting for twenty-seven years, and opened it to a blank page.

She didn't draw anything. Not yet.

She just held the pencil and looked at the white space.

For the first time in longer than she could even remember, there was a small, terrifying thrill of not knowing what came next.

CHAPTER 5

Harper's alarm clock went off at 4:45 a.m. For the first few seconds, she thought about quitting this whole pact thing, moving to Switzerland, and changing her name before these women could find her.

But she got up because Harper Ellis never quit. She quit people occasionally. Sometimes she quit relationships and hobbies, even a pottery class she had signed up for in a moment of weakness, but she did not quit commitments she had signed her name to, even if the commitment was written in bleeding ink on a dusty rose napkin and the result was nothing more than disappointing two women she loved.

Now that she thought about it, that was really the worst consequence she could imagine.

She made coffee in her Charleston condo. The machine was a $1,200 Italian model that produced espresso so good it was practically criminal. She only knew how to use two of the ten functions, and her now fifty-year-old brain had no desire to learn more.

The condo was on the fifth floor of the building with a view of the harbor that she paid a small fortune for but rarely looked at.

It was beautiful. It was immaculate. It had exactly one houseplant, a fiddle leaf fig that her assistant James watered on Wednesdays because Harper kept forgetting to.

The plant's survival was, in many ways, a testament to James rather than Harper. He was patient and wanted the plant to live a full life. She, on the other hand, didn't care what happened to the plant.

She drank her espresso standing at the kitchen island because she didn't have a kitchen table. She had meant to buy one. Actually, she had meant to buy one for over four years, since the day she moved in.

But every time she looked at tables online, she would think about who was going to sit at it, and the answer was always just her. So she would close the browser, eat standing up, and try to move on with her life.

Her phone buzzed. It was a text from Claire.

I'm picking up Nina at 5:30. We'll meet you at Folly by 6:15. Please tell me you didn't forget.

Harper:

I've been awake since 4:45. Trust me, I haven't forgotten. I'm regretting this already, but I have not forgotten.

Claire:

Wear something warm. It's December.

Harper:

I'm aware of the calendar, Claire.

Claire:

Bring towels.

Harper:

I know how to prepare for things. This is literally my profession.

Claire:

Okay, bring EXTRA towels.

Harper put her phone down and looked out the window. Charleston was still dark, the harbor a flat black plane dotted with boat lights.

In a couple of hours, she was going to run into the Atlantic Ocean in December on purpose because she had picked this adventure.

Because karaoke night had set the standard, and now Harper's competitive nature would not allow her to follow it with something tame.

So in the back of her mind, she thought, *if I'm going to feel something, it might as well be freezing water.* Of course, she had not said that part out loud, because she was not even ready to admit to Claire or Nina that she was searching for some kind of feeling in her life.

Her life was lonely in ways she had a hard time describing. It wasn't just her empty apartment. It was the way she moved through her day with such precision that there was no room for anything unplanned, no gap in the schedule where a feeling might sneak through.

Her calendar was full. Her life was full. Oh yes, it was full of meetings, strategy sessions, quarterly reviews, and working dinners.

But all of it added up to a life that looked very

impressive from the outside and felt like eating toast over the sink from the inside.

The morning prior to the plunge, Harper sat at her desk and had lunch.

This wasn't unusual for her.

She had lunch at her desk most days, a salad from the place on Broad Street that knew her order, shoveled into her mouth between emails while the city moved on without her.

Her office was on the fourteenth floor with a view of the steeple of St. Philip's Church, and she had earned every square foot of it through her twenty-two years of being sharper, smarter, and more prepared than anyone else in the room, including the men.

James appeared in her doorway around twelve. He was twenty-eight, immaculately dressed, and the only person in the company who didn't seem to be afraid of her.

He held a paper bag from the salad place in one hand and his cell phone in the other.

"Your mother called," he said.

"How many times?"

"Three."

"What did she want?"

"She said, and I quote, 'Tell my daughter that her cousin Margaux had her second child, and I'm not saying anything. I'm just telling her.'"

Harper closed her eyes. "Thank you, James," she said with a sigh.

"Oh, she also said that there's a cardiothoracic surgeon at her church who's recently divorced."

"Of course there is."

"She said he's very tall."

"Height has nothing to do with personality, James."

"I told her you were in a meeting, and she said she would call you back around two."

"Then I will be in a meeting at two."

"But you don't have anything at two."

"Then schedule something."

James gave her a look that was part sympathy and part amusement. He was very perceptive for someone his age.

He set the salad on her desk and left while Harper sat there in her corner office on the fourteenth floor and thought about her mother and cousin Margaux's second child and all the tall divorced surgeons who were probably very nice but very boring and would want to talk about their boat.

Eloise Ellis had been a Charleston society fixture

for forty years. She chaired fundraisers. She wore pearls to the grocery store.

She had married Harper's father at twenty-two years old, had Harper at twenty-four, and then buried Harper's father at fifty-eight years old and had spent all the years since maintaining the social calendar of a woman half her age and the disapproval of a mother who had expected grandchildren by now.

She didn't say it to her directly. She talked around everything. Eloise never said anything directly.

She would say things like, 'I'm not saying anything, I'm just telling you,' which was just her Charleston way of saying everything while maintaining plausible deniability.

She talked about other people's grandchildren the way a meteorologist might mention an approaching storm, factually, repeatedly, and with the clear implication that something should be done about it.

Harper ate her salad and did not call her mother back.

At 1:47, her phone rang.

It wasn't her mom.

It was Jordan.

She stared at the screen. It had been three weeks

since his birthday call. She had told herself he wouldn't call her again.

She had told Claire and Nina that she had handled it. Her phone rang a second time and then a third.

Harper's thumb hovered over the screen. She let it go to voicemail.

Then she sat in her office and didn't listen to the voicemail for the rest of the afternoon, which required a particular kind of discipline that, thankfully, Harper was very, very good at.

Folly Beach at 6:15 a.m. in December looked like the end of the world. The sky was just starting to lighten up with a thin line of gray and blue along the horizon.

The beach was empty except for a few joggers and one man with a metal detector, who clearly looked like he was living his best life. He had a small stack of metal objects piled up near a folding chair.

The ocean was dark and huge, and the air coming off of it had the kind of cold that did not just touch your skin but moved straight through it, settling into your bones.

Claire's car was already in the lot.

Harper found them at the edge of the dunes, Claire in a puffy coat and sneakers, holding a tote bag that probably had a thermos, extra towels, and some kind of organizational system.

Nina was beside her, wearing David's old windbreaker, her hands in her pockets, looking at the water.

"You brought towels?" Claire asked.

Harper groaned. "I brought towels."

"Extra towels?"

"Claire, I brought six towels, a change of clothes, a big thermos full of hot chocolate, and a separate thermos of hot chocolate with some bourbon in it. I'm prepared."

"And which one has the… which thermos has the bourbon?" Nina asked in a whisper.

"The red one."

"Well, giving it to you now would defeat the purpose," Claire said.

"Yeah, well, giving it to me now would ensure I actually get in the water," Nina said.

They stood at the edge of the dunes and looked out at the Atlantic. It was enormous, and it was for sure freezing.

Harper had to admit that this was completely insane, even though she had been the one to suggest it, which meant she had no one to blame but herself and possibly the second glass of wine she had been drinking when she had texted the group chat about a polar plunge at Folly Beach at dawn.

Claire had replied, "Define polar plunge," and Harper had replied, "Well, we run into the ocean in December as fast as we can."

Nina had replied, "I'm going to die," to which Harper had replied, "That's the spirit."

"Okay," Claire said.

She pulled three bathing suits out of her tote bag. They were matching, navy blue with white polka dots.

They all had retro cuts that suggested Claire had given this entirely too much thought.

"Wait a minute. You seriously bought us matching bathing suits?" Harper said.

"Yeah, I found them at Dedrick's. They were on sale."

"Claire Morrison, you did not buy matching bathing suits for a polar plunge because they were on sale. You bought them because you just cannot resist coordinating things."

"Well, both could be true."

Nina took hers and held it up. "David's mother is going to see photos of this and have an absolute panic attack."

"Elena will survive," Claire said.

"Elena will show up at my house with a casserole and then lecture me about pneumonia."

They changed in Claire's car, which involved a serious level of contortion that should not have been required of three fifty-year-old women at 6:30 in the morning.

Harper got her arms stuck in the seatbelt while trying to pull her top off over her head.

Claire accidentally honked the horn with her elbow, and Nina laughed so hard that she fogged up the windows.

They walked to the water's edge in matching navy polka dots and bare feet. The sand was cold, and the wind was colder. Thinking about putting their bodies in it seemed insane.

"Rules," Claire said, because Claire was not going to enter any body of water without establishing a firm protocol first."We go in together, we go in up to our waist at least, we stay in for thirty seconds."

"Thirty seconds?" Nina said. "That seems a little long. It's half a minute in freezing water. Half a minute is a lifetime, you know."

"Oh, come on, we can do thirty seconds," Harper said. "I sit through board meetings that feel longer than thirty seconds in the Atlantic."

They linked arms, three women in matching bathing suits at dawn on Folly Beach, the sky turning pink at the edges and the ocean seeming to wait for them.

"On the count of three," Claire said.

Harper braced herself. "On three."

"One," Nina said.

Claire shivered. "Two."

And then nobody said three.

They just ran like they were running for their lives, like an ax murderer was chasing them.

The water hit Harper's feet first, and it was so cold that it did not even feel cold. It felt like she had been shocked with electricity. It felt like she had been slapped awake by the entire Atlantic Ocean and all the fish in it.

It seemed like the ocean was not impressed by three women in polka dots.

She gasped. Claire screamed.

Nina made a sound that sounded somewhere between a war cry and a prayer.

They kept running and splashing through the shallows, the water climbing their legs, their thighs, their waists, and Harper's whole body was screaming.

Her brain was also screaming that she had lost her mind. Beneath all the screaming, a feeling she had not felt in years remained.

She was awake. Completely, entirely, and shockingly awake. Not the type of caffeine and willpower awake that she normally ran on every day.

This was different. This was every nerve in her body firing at once. Every cell suddenly remembered it was alive.

The cold was brutal and magnificent as they stood waist-deep in the December Atlantic, throwing their heads back and laughing.

Claire started counting. Of course, Claire was counting.

"Fifteen! Sixteen! Seventeen!"

Nina was shaking. Her teeth were chattering so loud they could almost hear it over the waves. Out of the three of them, Nina was the petite one. Over the last year, she'd lost weight, and Harper worried the cold would snap her little bones in half soon.

Nina's arms were wrapped around herself, but she was grinning, not smiling, grinning. The full, silly grin of a woman who had just remembered that her body could do things besides grieving.

"Twenty-five! Twenty-six!"

"I can't feel my legs anymore!" Nina shouted.

"That's how you know it's working!" Harper shouted back.

"Thirty!" Claire yelled.

They turned and ran back through the shallows, stumbling and splashing, half falling onto the beach, where they collapsed in a pile of wet polka dots and laughter so big that it echoed off the dunes.

After being in the freezing cold ocean, the hot chocolate tasted like a religious experience. They sat in the open back of Claire's SUV with their legs dangling, towels hanging around their shoulders, passing the thermoses back and forth.

The parking lot was still pretty empty. A few more early morning joggers had appeared.

The man with the metal detector had moved farther down the beach, searching for whatever it was that made people get out of bed at dawn to sweep the sand with an electric stick.

The sun was fully up now, and Folly Beach looked like a postcard.

Harper took a long drink from the thermos. The bourbon and chocolate hit her chest like a warm hug, and she closed her eyes.

She was wet and cold and sitting in a parking lot at seven o'clock in the morning in a bathing suit, but she felt more alive than she had felt in her corner office for years.

"I have a question," Nina said. She was holding

Claire's thermos with both hands, her dark hair dripping onto the towel. "Who picks month three?"

"Well, we should just keep the rotation," Claire said, because there was no way that Claire was going to have an unstructured situation. "You picked month one, Harper picked month two, so I pick month three."

"Well, then what?"

"Then we just cycle back to Nina, Harper, Claire. Four rounds of three, twelve months."

Harper nodded.

"A very organized rotation, Claire."

"Well, I am a third-grade teacher, so organization is kind of my thing. I could get us in a single-file line like that!" She snapped her fingers.

"You organized the karaoke song list by genre before we even got over to the bar."

"Oh, that was just basic categorization," Claire said, waving her hand.

"Claire, you made a spreadsheet."

"Spreadsheets are important to life."

Nina laughed.

It was becoming a regular thing to hear Nina laugh again.

Harper liked it. She liked seeing Nina with her hair down, Nina getting into the car without sitting in the driveway for ten minutes first.

"I have an idea for month three," Claire said.

Before she could say it, Nina shook her head. "Wait, actually, can I just go out of order?"

Claire and Harper both looked at her.

"But the rotation—"

"I know the rotation says it's Claire's turn," Nina said, "but I have something, something I've been thinking about since our birthday dinner, and if I don't say it right now, I'm going to talk myself out of it."

Harper recognized that voice. It was the voice Nina used when something really mattered, so much that she could barely get it out, like when she told them she was pregnant with Lucia, or the same voice she used on the phone the morning David died.

"Go ahead," Harper said.

Nina was looking out at the ocean, which felt like it had nearly killed them about twenty minutes ago.

"A cooking class. Oaxacan food. David's grand-mother's recipes. There's a woman in North Charleston, Señora Morales. Anyway, she teaches out of her home kitchen. She's from the same region as David's family. Elena told me about her months ago, and I just kept meaning to sign up, but I never did."

She paused.

"I was too scared because… Going there felt like

admitting I needed to learn the things David already knew, like the recipes he grew up with and the food his grandmother made. He was the one who always cooked that stuff. He was the one who carried on that part of his family, and learning them from a stranger felt like admitting he's really gone and that somebody else has to teach me now. Like maybe I didn't take the time to learn from my soulmate before he was gone."

Nobody spoke.

A pelican dove into the surf, and Harper thought of David, who had been exactly that kind of man, all heart, no pretension, bobbing down and getting the fish every time.

"But I promised Lucia," Nina continued. "I promised her that I would write it all down. David's recipes, Elena's recipes, everything. But I can't write down what I don't know." She looked at Claire and then at Harper. "So that's my pick, if you'll let me go out of turn."

Harper reached over and took the thermos from Nina. Not because she wanted a drink, but because she wanted Nina's hands free so she could hold them.

Harper Ellis, who touched people the way cats touch water, held Nina's cold, wet hands.

"You don't need anybody's permission to go out of turn. It's your pact, too."

"We're there," Claire said. "You just tell us when. And I think this pact only works if we let each other get what we need out of it. There's no right way to do it."

"Did Claire Morrison just say there's no right way to do something?" Harper said, smiling.

"Don't tell anybody I said that. Also," Claire said, "I cannot cook Oaxacan food. I burn rice. I will be the worst student Señora Morales has ever had in her kitchen."

"That's fine," Nina said. "I think that's part of the adventure."

"Burning rice is not an adventure. It's a fire hazard." Harper smiled.

She looked at her two best friends, each of them wrapped in towels and shivering in a parking lot. But she could feel something changing inside of her.

She picked up her phone under the towel where nobody could see and listened to Jordan's message. His voice was the same, warm and unhurried, the voice of a man who never rushed through anything.

"Hey, Harper, it's me. Listen, I know it's been a while. I just wanted to say a belated happy birthday. I know I'm really late. I hope fifty is treating you well."

Then a pause.

There was a sound in the background, maybe a saw or a sander.

"I think about you sometimes. I hope that's okay. Anyway, you know where to find me."

Harper listened to it twice and then tucked her phone back under the towel. She pulled her towel tighter around her shoulders and watched the sun finish rising.

She didn't call him back, not yet. But not yet was different from never.

CHAPTER 6

Señora Morales lived in a pale yellow house on a side street in North Charleston. She had an overgrown garden that looked like it could feed the entire neighborhood.

The front yard was a barely controlled mound of herbs, peppers, and flowering plants that Nina definitely could not name. Plants climbed to the porch railing and spilled over into clay pots.

A hand-painted sign by the mailbox read "Cocina de Morales," in letters that were a little crooked and very confident.

The house smelled, even from the driveway, like toasted chilies and something sweet. The smell hit Nina in the chest. David's kitchen used to smell like this.

Not often because David was just a weekend

cook, a man who spent Monday through Friday eating whatever was fast and then devoted Saturday mornings to the long, patient work of his grand-mother's recipes.

Mole that took five hours, tamales that took seven, black beans that simmered all day on the back burner while he played music too loud and danced with Lucia on his hips, her little hands covered in masa, both of them laughing at nothing and at everything.

Nina sat in the car for a moment. At least it was not forty-five minutes, not even ten.

Just a moment long enough to breathe in that smell and decide how she was going to walk into this house without falling apart.

Claire knocked on the passenger window.

"You okay?"

"I'm okay."

"You sure?"

"I'm sure. I'm coming."

Harper was already on the porch, looking at the herb garden as if she were gathering data for a spreadsheet. She picked a leaf off something and sniffed it. "This is epazote," she said.

"And how do you know that?" Claire said.

"I researched Oaxacan cuisine last night. You know I like to be prepared for things."

"You researched for a cooking class?"

"I research everything. Knowledge is power, Claire."

"It's just beans and rice, not like we're doing a hostile takeover of a corporation."

The front door opened before Harper could say anything, and Señora Morales appeared.

She was small. Actually, she was tiny. That was the very first thing Nina noticed.

She was smaller than Elena, which Nina did not even think was possible.

She was maybe five feet tall in the slippers she wore, her silver-streaked black hair pulled back in a braid, and her brown skin shaped by decades of sun and laughter.

She wore a simple apron over a blue cotton dress. Her eyes were dark and warm, the eyes of a woman who could look at you once and tell whether you had even eaten breakfast. Much like Elena.

"You must be Nina." Her accent was thicker than Elena's. "Elena told me about you. She said you were ready."

Nina did not know what Elena had told this woman. Knowing Elena, she had told her every-thing, down to Nina's shoe size and astrological sign.

She had definitely told her about the marriage,

the death, the grief, the frozen waffles, and the parking lots.

Elena did not believe in privacy when it came to family, and she considered Nina her family for life. That meant Nina's business was Elena's business, which was now apparently Señora Morales' business.

"These are my friends," Nina said. "Claire and Harper."

Señora Morales looked at Claire, then at Harper, and then back at Nina.

"They cook?"

"Claire bakes," Nina said. "I mean, Harper mostly just orders food and people bring it to her."

"I can cook," Harper said, obviously feeling under the microscope. This, of course, was said with the confidence of a woman who had only ever made pasta from a box.

Señora Morales smiled. "Come in. We start with the chili."

The kitchen was very small, but it was immaculate. Most importantly, it was alive. Every surface had something on it.

Molcajetes in three sizes lined up on the counter.

Big bundles of dried chilies hanging from hooks near a window. A comal on the stove that was so well seasoned, it was nearly black.

Stacks of big clay bowls in colors that reminded Nina of the pottery David used to buy whenever they visited his cousins in Oaxaca.

A radio on the windowsill played something soft and acoustic, barely audible amid the sound of Señora Morales moving around her kitchen.

There were four stations set up along a long wooden table that served as a workspace and a dining surface. Cutting boards, bowls of ingredients, knives, and a small stack of index cards with hand-written recipes in Spanish. Señora Morales had translated them into English underneath in very small letters.

"Today we make three things," she said, tying on an apron like she was preparing for battle. "First, we make salsa de pasilla. Simple. It's very good for beginners." She looked at Harper. "Good for people who like to order in."

"Oh, wow, I feel seen," Harper said, putting a hand to her chest.

"Secondly, we make tortillas by hand. We're not using a machine. Your hands learn the masa, or the tortilla is just bread."

"And what's the third thing?" Claire asked, studying the index cards.

Señora Morales looked at Nina. "Mole negro."

The kitchen went silent.

It wasn't because anyone understood the weight of the words, but because Nina did, and they could see the look on her face.

Mole negro was David's favorite dish.

It was the recipe his grandmother had brought from Oaxaca to the United States in the sixties, written on a piece of paper that was so thin you could see through it.

It had been passed down to his mother, then to David, who spent 20 years perfecting it. He used to say that mole was not a sauce, it was a conversation between thirty ingredients, and they all had to learn to get along.

"Elena gave me the recipe," Señora Morales said quietly. "Your husband's family recipe. She said it was time someone else learned it."

Nina's throat felt tight. She nodded because she couldn't form words. She felt Claire's hand on her back.

"We start," Señora Morales said matter-of-factly. She wasn't unkind, but she was firm. Like many women of her age, there was no time to sit and stew over the things a person cannot change. There was only time to get on with it. "The chilies first. They need to toast."

She handed each of them a dried pasilla chili. The skin was dark and papery, almost black. Nina held it to her nose. It smelled like smoke and earth.

David used to buy these by the pound at a shop on Rivers Avenue. He would come home with bags of dried chilies and spread them across the kitchen counter. Then he would sort them by type with seriousness.

"You hold it over the comal," Señora Morales demonstrated, pressing the chili flat against the very hot surface with her bare fingers. Claire was visibly nervous. "You count to ten, you flip, you count to ten again. When it blisters and the smell changes, it's ready. But don't burn it. Burnt chili is an angry chili, and angry chili will ruin everything."

"Wow, that feels like a metaphor," Harper said, nodding. "I think I'm an angry chili," she said under her breath.

"It is a chili," Señora Morales said flatly. "Not everything is a metaphor."

They toasted chilies. Nina went first, pressing the pasilla to the comal and counting under her breath the way David used to. The smell filled the kitchen, smoky and sharp. It was so familiar that her hands started to shake, but she didn't cry.

She just pressed the chili, counted, flipped, counted, and placed it in the bowl that Señora Morales held out. Her hands were shaking but steady, if that was even possible.

Claire toasted hers carefully and precisely, turning it exactly at ten seconds. She loved to follow directions to the letter.

Harper approached it the way she approached everything: with confidence, speed, and a slight overestimation of her own abilities.

She burned her first chili.

"Angry chili," Señora Morales said, taking it from her.

"Well, I counted to ten."

"Yes, but you counted to ten very fast. Chili does not care about your schedule."

Nina laughed.

She felt it coming before she heard it, like a bubble rising through that tightening in her chest that had been there for so many months.

It surprised even her, because she had been so sure this morning that this was going to be hard. She had braced herself for all the pain of it and forgotten to account for the possibility that it might also be enjoyable and even funny, that David's food could bring her joy and grief in the same breath, and that she could allow both to exist in the same kitchen.

The tortillas were an absolute disaster.

Señora Morales mixed the masa with warm water and worked it in her hands until it reached a consistency that she could only describe as being "like a baby's cheek," which was the most specific and least helpful cooking instruction Claire had ever received in her entire life.

She handed each of them a ball of dough and a tortilla press, then stepped back to watch.

She had probably seen hundreds of people fail at this and found it both amusing and educational.

Claire's first tortilla was way too thick. Her second was so thin it had holes in it. Her third was a shape that could only be described as oval, but was more accurately a huge mistake.

She was concentrating so hard that a small line had appeared between her eyebrows. It was the same line she got when she was grading papers or trying to do any other task that required full, meticulous attention.

"You think too much," Señora Morales told her. "Tortillas don't want you to think. They want you to feel."

"Well, I'm not very good at that," Claire said. She

meant the tortilla, but the words came out carrying more weight than she probably intended.

Harper's tortillas were pretty decent, surprisingly.

She pressed the dough with decisive force, like she brought to everything, and the results were round and even and quite competent, which was the word for most things that Harper produced.

"Natural talent," Harper said, holding one up. "It's a circle."

"Most preschoolers can do that," Nina said, laughing.

"It's a perfect circle. Geometry matters."

Nina's tortillas were uneven and a little too thick, but they were exactly right. Her hands seemed to know how to do something her brain didn't. The dough felt familiar, even though she had never done this a day in her life.

It was as if she had muscle memory that had been waiting for her, inherited over years of watching her husband, of standing next to him in their kitchen as he pressed and flipped and sang along to whatever was playing on the radio.

Señora Morales watched Nina. "Elena was right. You do have good hands."

"Elena said that?"

"Oh, Elena said many things. Most of them are correct."

They cooked tortillas on the comal, watching them puff and blister, the smell of toasted corn filling the kitchen.

Nina thought about all those mornings when David made tortillas for breakfast, standing at the stove in his boxers and a T-shirt, the one with holes in it, flipping them with his fingers because he said a spatula was for people who didn't trust their own hands.

She ate one warm tortilla off the comal with nothing on it. It tasted like earth and corn and the ghost of those hundreds of Saturday mornings. She closed her eyes and let herself travel to that place where everything had been right in the world.

The mole took two whole hours.

Señora Morales guided them confidently, as someone who had done this countless times.

Toast the chilies, soak the chilies, roast the tomatoes and tomatillos, fry the tortilla pieces until they are dark and crispy, toast the spices, cumin, clove, black pepper, oregano, roast the garlic, blend everything in stages because mole was not a recipe that you could rush and throw everything together.

According to Señora Morales, it was an insult to the ingredients.

The chocolate went in last: two tablets of Mexican chocolate, dark, grainy, and sweet, dropped into the pot, where they melted slowly into the sauce, turning it from a dark red to a deep brown that was almost black.

The kitchen smelled like everything that was good in the world, the kind of smell that made you want to sit down and not get up again for a very long time.

Nina stirred the mole. Señora Morales had given her a spoon and then stepped back.

Claire and Harper stepped back, too, so that Nina stood at the stove alone.

She stirred the sauce that David's grandmother had made in a kitchen in Oaxaca sixty years ago, that David's mother had made in a kitchen in Charleston for thirty years, that David had made in their kitchen for years, and that Nina was now making in a stranger's kitchen in Charleston, her hands shaking, her heart broken, with her two best friends who loved her enough to just stand in the corner and let her do this.

The smell of chocolate and chilies rose up and

permeated the room. Nina stirred, and the tears came. She didn't want to stop stirring.

They ran down her face and dropped into the pot, and she thought David would have said it was fine, that the best mole has a little salt, that food with tears was made with love.

Nobody said anything.

Claire put her hand over her mouth, and Harper just stood there still with her arms crossed. Señora Morales watched from the doorway.

She had seen grief walk through this kitchen before. That much was obvious. And she knew the best thing to do was just let it happen.

Nina stirred.

The mole thickened and darkened.

It looked like something David would have been really proud of. She could hear his voice in her head.

Stir slower, mi amor. You're rushing it. Let it talk to you.

So she stirred more slowly. She let it talk. After a while, she stopped crying.

Not because her grief was gone, but because it had somewhere to go now. It was in the mole.

It was in the chilies and chocolate and hours of slow, patient work.

Standing at that stove, she understood that this

was what David had meant when he said cooking was a conversation.

This conversation with food and the people who made it for you, and with yourself, was so important, and it didn't end when you finished cooking.

It just got quieter.

Señora Morales walked to the stove. She took a small spoon and dipped it in the mole, tasting it. She closed her eyes and then opened them.

"Your husband taught you something after all," she said, a smile on her face.

"Well, no, he never taught me this recipe."

"Nobody taught you how to cook with your heart. The recipe is just the directions, the words. The heart is what makes it food." She handed Nina a stack of index cards. "Write everything down, all of this, the way I showed you and the way you felt. And then you can give it to your daughter one day, and she can give it to hers."

Nina took the cards. Her hands were steady as a rock now.

They sat together and ate at Señora Morales's kitchen table. It was crowded, but it was warm, and it felt like they were all inside their own little hug.

They ate mole over rice. They ate beautiful but imperfect tortillas. The salsa de pasilla that Harper had redeemed herself on after the angry chili incident was also a winner.

Señora Morales brought out cold bottles of Jarritos and a plate of sliced mango with chili powder. They sat, ate, and talked for what seemed like hours.

Señora Morales told them about her own husband, who had passed away eleven years ago. He loved to fish but hated to cook, and once tried to make mole from a jar, only to be nearly banished from the house.

She told them about coming to Charleston from Oaxaca in 1989 with only $200 and a suitcase full of dried chilies because she was afraid she could not get them in America.

She told them that cooking for other people was how she stayed close to the people she had lost, because food was memory made physical. As long as someone was eating your recipe, then the person who taught it to you was still alive in some way.

Nina listened and ate. She felt full in a way that had nothing to do with food.

She was full in her chest and her hands, and in

that part of herself that had been so hollow for a year and a half, that was slowly and carefully starting to come alive again.

Claire's phone rang during dessert. She glanced over at it, and Nina saw her face change a bit. It wasn't dramatic, but just a small tightening around her mouth.

"Sorry," Claire said, standing up. "I need to take this." She stepped out onto Señora Morales's porch and closed the door behind her.

Through the window, Nina could see Claire pacing back and forth. She had one hand on the back of her neck, which was a tell that Claire was stressed.

She was speaking in a low, careful voice, the one she usually used with her husband when things were tense. And over the past couple of months, that seemed to be happening more and more often.

Harper had noticed it too. She watched Claire through the window for a moment, but then turned back to the table.

"Greg?" Nina asked quietly.

"Yeah, I'm thinking Greg," Harper confirmed.

Señora Morales looked at the porch, then at Harper, and then at Nina. She said nothing. She was the kind of woman who understood that some conversations were not hers to join.

Claire returned about five minutes later and sat down. She picked up her drink. She smiled the smile Nina knew too well, the one that said, don't worry, I'm fine, please don't ask.

So Nina did not ask, and neither did Harper. Of course, they would later, in the car or on the phone or maybe on Claire's porch with some wine, which was where the three of them did their real talking.

But not here.

Not in Señora Morales's kitchen, where the mole was still warm on their plates.

"Everything okay?" Nina asked, which was not really the same thing as asking what was wrong.

Claire knew the difference.

"Greg just wanted to know when I'd be home." She took another sip of her drink. "He said I'm never home anymore."

The table went quiet.

"And what did you say?" Harper asked.

"I said I'd be home when I was done." She looked at her hands. They were still dusty with masa flour, and dried chili sat under her fingernails. "He didn't ask how I was doing. He doesn't really care about that kind of thing. He just wanted to know when I would be back. Probably to cook dinner."

Harper set down her fork. Her jaw did that thing it did when it was holding back something sharp.

Nina could see the words lining up behind Harper's teeth.

He doesn't deserve you.

He hasn't noticed you in twenty years.

Why are you still counting to three before you say what you really think?

But Harper did not say any of that, because Harper, despite all her sharpness, knew when a friend just needed space more than they needed truth. So she reached over and squeezed Claire's hand.

"Let's clean up," Señora Morales said, rising from the table. She was a woman with authority, redirecting the room. "And then I will send you home with enough mole for your families. Then you'll come back, and we will make tamales another day." She looked at Nina. "Your mother-in-law will expect tamales."

"Oh, my mother-in-law expects everything," Nina said.

They cleaned the kitchen together, washing dishes, wiping counters, putting things back in their places.

Claire dried the bowls carefully.

Harper organized the spice jars by height because Harper could never help herself.

Nina swept the floor and found, near the leg of

the table, a small dollop of chocolate from the mole. She wiped it up with her finger and thought about this being the best day she had had in so long.

The drive home was quieter than normal. Claire drove, and Harper sat in the passenger seat with a container of mole balanced on her lap.

Somehow, she had managed the entire day without staining her beautiful silk blouse. It was a miracle. Nina considered it evidence of either the divine or of Harper's sheer force of will.

Nina sat in the back with two containers, one for herself, one for Elena, because Señora Morales had insisted and because Nina wanted Elena to taste it.

She wanted Elena to know that someone else had taught her the recipe, that it was okay, and that the food hadn't been lost when David died. It was still here, in a little kitchen in North Charleston, in Nina's hands, and on index cards that she would one day give to her daughter.

The late-afternoon sun slanted through the windshield as they crossed the Ashley River. Claire's knuckles were white on the steering wheel, telling Nina more than any words could.

"You know, you don't have to talk about it," Nina said from the backseat, "but you can if you want."

Claire was quiet for a long stretch of the road. They passed live oaks draped in moss, shadows across the asphalt.

"He's not wrong," Claire finally said. "I am gone a lot more than I used to be. Three Saturdays in a row now. I went shopping alone last Saturday, and I went to that new book club the Saturday before that."

"Well, you're allowed to leave your house on a Saturday, Claire. It's not like you're going out on dates with other men," Harper said, looking over at her.

"I know that."

"Do you?"

Claire didn't answer. The road curved through a stretch of marsh.

"He used to ask me where I was going," Claire said. "You know, years ago, he'd ask, and I'd tell him, and he'd say, 'Oh, have fun.' Now he doesn't say anything. He doesn't ask where I'm going. He just asks when I'm coming back. There's a difference there."

Nina understood the difference. One indicated interest, and the other just indicated someone taking inventory. One said, I care about your life. The other said, I need to know when my life goes back to normal.

"What do you want to do about it?" Nina asked quietly.

"I don't know. I honestly don't know."

The way she said it, quiet and honestly bewildered, told Nina this was the truest thing Claire had said about her marriage in years. She didn't seem angry or sad.

She just seemed genuinely confused, because she was a woman who had spent twenty-six years building something and was now starting to realize she didn't know what she'd built or even how strong it was.

They dropped Harper at her building in Charleston. Then Claire drove Nina to Edisto, and the road narrowed to two lanes. Nina got out of the car with her containers, but she leaned back through the window.

"Claire?"

"Yeah?"

"You know what Señora Morales said about the tortilla? That you don't want to think, that it wants you to feel?" Claire just looked at her. "Well, anyway, maybe that's not just about the tortillas."

She didn't wait for Claire to respond. She just

squeezed her arm through the window and walked up the porch steps, the marsh singing its night song as Nina walked into her kitchen and put the mole on the counter.

She called Elena. She answered on the first ring, which meant she had been sitting there waiting.

"So how was it?" Elena asked.

"I made the mole, Elena."

A silence settled. Nina could hear Elena's shallow breaths, imagining her in her modest house surrounded by little saints on the shelf and photos of David adorning every wall.

"Was it good?"

"Señora Morales said David taught me something after all."

Elena made a noise that was neither quite a laugh nor a cry. It was the sound of a mother hearing her deceased son's name spoken with affection by someone gradually learning to honor his memory.

"I'll bring you some tomorrow," Nina said.

"Bring Lucia," Elena said. "We'll eat together."

"Okay."

"And Nina?"

"Yeah?"

"Good girl."

Elena hung up because she didn't believe in long goodbyes.

Nina stood in her kitchen holding her phone, next to the mole on the counter, feeling like she was finally in the right place for once.

CHAPTER 7

The confrontation, when it eventually appeared, wasn't truly a fight. It was just an ordinary Tuesday. Claire was preparing dinner because that was her usual routine.

Over twenty-six years of marriage, the division of labor became an unspoken arrangement that nobody explicitly agreed to, yet everyone adhered to.

Claire cooked.

Greg ate.

Claire cleaned up.

Greg went to the den.

It was their system. Systems generally didn't need debate; they just operated until someone disconnected them or they failed completely.

She was chopping onions when Greg opened his mouth.

"You're doing it again this Saturday?"

She continued chopping. The onion made her eyes water, which was helpful because it gave her tears somewhere to hide.

"Doing what?"

"The thing with Harper and Nina. Your new little club."

Little club.

He spoke of it as if calling it a 'little hobby' or 'little phase,' to belittle her and dismiss her, as if the most significant thing Claire achieved in the past decade could be reduced to something small enough to fit in a word like 'little.'

"We're going rock climbing," she said, "at a gym in Charleston. It should be fun."

"Rock climbing? You three?" Greg leaned against the counter and crossed his arms. This was his posture when delivering opinions he thought were reasonable but that nobody asked for. "You're fifty years old, Claire."

"Yes, I'm aware of my age. I was there when it happened."

"I'm just saying you've been gone a lot lately. Karaoke, that thing y'all did at the beach, the cooking thing at that lady's house. Seems like it's always something new."

"Well, the 'cooking whatever' was a cooking class. I learned to make mole, and it took hours. And I have to say, it was one of the best days I've had in many years." She hadn't actually meant to say that last part.

It came out before she could catch it, and then it landed on the kitchen counter between them like somebody had dropped it from a very tall height.

One of the best days I've had in years.

Not a day that included her husband.

Not a day that included her sitting at home.

But a day with her best friends in a stranger's kitchen, learning something new.

Greg's face did a thing she'd seen before but never named.

He didn't look angry or hurt. It was a bit like confusion, or maybe bewilderment from a man who had been living in the same house as her for twenty-six years and was just now realizing that one of the rooms had a door he'd never opened.

"Well, I didn't say you couldn't go," he said.

"I know you didn't. And you don't get to make that decision for me anyway."

"I'm just saying it feels like a lot."

Claire set the knife down on the counter. She

looked at her husband. He was wearing the same old College of Charleston T-shirt he'd had since before they were married, which was now very soft and faded. He wore it a lot, now that she thought about it. He had a closet full of clothes, yet he always wore that shirt.

His hair was graying at the temples. This was the face that she had fallen in love with. The same face she had thought she couldn't live without at twenty-three years old. But now it was older and quieter and getting further away.

"It's just one Saturday a month, Greg."

"It seems like every Saturday."

"No, it's one. One Saturday. Twenty-six years of Saturdays, and I'm asking for twelve of them for myself."

"You've been going other places, too."

She stared at him like he'd grown a second head. "And? You have a problem with me enjoying myself at Target? Or spending the day talking about books with a few new friends?"

The counter between them felt heavier than it was. Greg looked at her, and she could see him trying to do the math, running through the numbers the way he did at work, trying to figure out when the equation in their marriage had changed and why things no longer seemed to balance.

"I just miss you," he said.

That should have softened her. A year ago, maybe it would have.

A year ago, maybe she would have put the knife down and walked across the kitchen and touched his arm and said, "I'm right here." And she would have meant it.

The moment might have faded, like many others, quietly dismissed and hidden. However, she was in a kitchen fragrant with onions, having spent several weekends feeling more vibrant than she had in ten years.

Her husband had just called the thing that was saving her a *little club*. And the words, *I just miss you*, sounded less like love and more like a man saying them out of obligation.

"Well, I miss me too, Greg," she said. "I miss the woman I used to be before I forgot who she was."

He didn't understand. She could see it on his face, the blankness, the genuine confusion of someone who was being spoken to in a language they didn't speak.

He stood there for a moment, his arms still crossed, and then said, "Well, hope you have fun," in the same tone he would use when she told him she was going to the grocery store to get eggs and toilet paper.

Then, unsurprisingly, he went back to the den. Claire stood in the kitchen alone.

That was it. That was the moment.

That was his chance, and he walked away from it.

She picked up the knife and finished chopping the onions. She made dinner, as usual, but she let the onions take the blame for all the tears.

Claire thought the climbing gym named Gravity was quite literal and possibly a bit intimidating. Gravity was what was likely to have her hanging upside down by her ankles within the hour.

It was located inside a converted warehouse on Upper King Street in Charleston, likely once a cotton mill, machine shop, or similar industrial building, before someone added colorful handholds to the walls and started charging people to climb on artificial rocks.

The walls were huge, stretching three stories high and covered in a rainbow of grips that looked like they had been designed by somebody who wanted to make physical exertion look more like a children's preschool classroom. They weren't fooling anyone. This place was intimidating.

Claire had picked this adventure because she wanted to do something with her body. The karaoke had been about her voice, and the plunge had been about the sensation. The cooking class had been about Nina's heart, really.

Claire wanted muscles, sweat, and the honest challenge of getting from the bottom to the top. She wanted to prove she could do something that had nothing to do with taking care of other people, something selfishly for herself. Of course, she had wanted all of that while she lounged in a bubble bath, not thinking of the repercussions.

Climbing a wall seemed to qualify for all of it. Of course, she had not mentioned to anyone that she was terrified of heights. She had somehow avoided telling that to either of her best friends for almost thirty years.

Harper and Nina were already in the lobby when she arrived. Harper was wearing new climbing shoes, clearly bought for this occasion, as she only owned well-fitting, purpose-built footwear.

Nina was wearing leggings and one of Lucia's old T-shirts that said Edisto Island Surf Club on it. That was funny because Edisto did not really have surfing, and Lucia had never been to a club in her life.

"Have either of you ever done this before?" Claire asked, staring at one of the walls.

"Nope," Nina said.

"I did watch a YouTube tutorial," Harper said, her index finger tapping her chin.

"Yeah, I don't think you can learn to climb a wall from YouTube," Claire responded.

"You can learn the principles. That's what matters. Knowing all the steps," Harper said, trying to convince herself.

Their instructor was a young man named Kai, who had the build of somebody who had been climbing since before he could walk. He also had the patience of someone who regularly taught terrified beginners like the three of them.

He showed them how to tie in, belay, and read the route. He explained the grading system. He also explained that falling was normal, expected, and that they should not be embarrassed about it.

"Everybody falls," he said cheerfully. "The wall is designed to make you fall. The question is, what do you do afterward?"

"Um, quit?" Claire offered. "Or cry? Maybe crying is better."

"No, you climb again," Kai said with the smiley confidence of a twenty-five-year-old who had never even reorganized a pantry alphabetically or chosen napkin colors for a birthday party. He hadn't lived yet. What did he know?

They started at the beginner wall. It was the shortest one in the gym, maybe twenty feet tall. It had large holds in primary colors that looked like they were begging to be grabbed. This was probably a wall that toddlers with strong forearms could climb. Surely it wouldn't be much of a challenge.

Nina went first because she was still riding the momentum of being the first, and it turns out she was pretty good at it. Not flashy, not fast even, just steady and methodical, taking one hold at a time.

She climbed the way she grieved, slowly and carefully, never letting go of one thing until she was sure she had a hold of the next one.

Harper went second and scaled the wall like she was late for a meeting at the top. Of course, she had the longest legs and arms out of the three of them. She was competitive and athletic, and this was how she approached everything: with speed and determination, and with absolutely no thought or interest in doing anything wrong.

She reached the top in what felt like thirty seconds and then looked down at them with an expression of satisfaction before rappelling back down as if she had been doing this her entire life.

"Your turn," Nina said to Claire.

Claire looked at the wall. Twenty feet. A rope

attached to her harness. Kai at the bottom, ready to grab her.

Everything was perfectly safe, all perfectly manageable, and all perfectly terrifying.

She put her hands on the first hold and started climbing. She was fine for the first ten feet, actually better than fine. It was as if her body remembered what her brain had forgotten.

How to stretch her arms and reach for things. The satisfaction of pulling yourself up. The physics of just regular weight and leverage.

She had been a gymnast in high school, which was now a lifetime ago. Somewhere deep in her muscles, the memory must have still lived. Dusty but functional, like a book she pulled from a shelf after thirty years. She could do this!

At about fifteen feet, she made the terrible mistake of looking down. The gym floor was right below her, further than it should have been.

Kai was a small figure holding a rope, while Harper and Nina looked up at her with tilted heads and mouths slightly open.

Now the wall seemed less like a fun challenge and more like a vertical surface that was actively trying to take her life. Yep, this was it. The news would say a poor fifty-year-old woman lost her life falling fifteen feet onto a padded floor because she panicked. What an embarrassing way to go out.

And when they asked her husband for a comment, he wouldn't have even realized she was gone until at least dinner time.

Claire's hands locked on the holds.

Her feet locked onto the footholds, and then her entire body said, "Nope."

She froze.

And not in the dramatic kind of freezing that happens in a movie where the character gasps, and the music swells. This was the quiet kind of freezing where all of your muscles suddenly stop cooperating. Your brain says move, and your body just says," That's going to be a no from me."

Claire hung on the wall fifteen feet up and couldn't go up or down or do anything but grip the hold so tightly that her knuckles went white. Her forearms started to burn. She could hear her heartbeat in her ears.

"Claire," Kai called up. "You okay?"

No, she was not okay. She was hanging on to this fake rock in a converted warehouse in Charleston, having what she would suspect was either a panic attack or a profound spiritual experience, and she couldn't tell the difference.

"Just take a breath," Nina said from below. Her

voice was calm and steady. She knew this was the same voice she used with Lucia when there were thunderstorms or she had had a bad dream as a kid. "You don't have to go up. You don't have to come down. Just breathe."

Claire breathed. It wasn't as if she hadn't been breathing the whole time, but for some reason she'd needed Nina's reminder.

The wall was cool under her hands. She could smell the chalk on her fingers. She could hear the gym around her, other climbers, the squeak of their shoes on the holds, someone laughing on the bouldering wall in the next section.

All normal and safe sounds. She was not going to die. She was just going to hang on this wall and breathe and figure out what to do next.

"Claire?" Harper called up. Her voice was quite a bit different from Nina's. More direct. It was the voice she always used in meetings when someone needed to make a decision and seemed to be stalling. "Listen, you have two choices. You can come down, and that's fine. We'll be proud of you for just trying. Or you can look at that next hold. Just the next one. Don't look up at the top. Don't look at the ground. Just look at the next hold and decide if you can reach it."

Claire looked at the next hold. It was blue, maybe

two feet above her right hand. It was shaped like a jug, which Kai had said was the easiest kind, and it was right there within her reach.

So she reached for it.

Her hand closed around the blue hold. She pulled hard, and her feet found the next foothold. And then she was moving again. It was definitely neither graceful nor fast. She probably looked like a monkey on espresso trying to get to that next hold.

Just one hold at a time, the way that she had seen Nina climb, the way Nina did everything now. Just one grip to the next. She didn't look down again. She didn't look up either.

She just looked at the next hold, then the next, then the next. The wall started to pass under her hands and feet.

The sounds of the gym faded, and there was nothing but her, the rock, the quiet, and the stubborn act of going up, even as everything in her wanted to let go.

Suddenly, her hand hit the top.

Claire Morrison, fifty years old, a third-grade teacher, napkin chooser, onion chopper, and wife of a man who watched the '95 Braves on repeat, touched the top of that climbing wall inside a converted warehouse in Charleston and burst into tears.

These weren't sad tears, not the kind that she swallowed for most of the last few years. These were the other kind, the kind that came from being proud of yourself when you haven't felt like feeling in years. Maybe decades.

She hung at the top of the wall and cried.

Below her, she could hear Nina clapping and Harper whistling.

"Get down here so I can hug you!" Nina shouted.

Claire rappelled down.

It was also shaky and graceless, and she did bump into the wall twice, almost knocking herself out. But when her feet hit the ground, Nina grabbed her and held on.

Then Harper grabbed both of them.

And the three of them stood in the climbing gym, chalky, sweating, crying, and laughing.

Kai just stood off to the side, looking pleased with himself and a little bit confused, which was probably his default expression when dealing with fifty-year-old women who were having emotional breakdowns and breakthroughs right in front of his beginner wall. Ah, to be twenty-five again. He had no idea what life would bring him.

The three women sat on a bench in the late-afternoon sun, drinking water and watching King Street do what it did on Saturdays.

It was filled with tourists with shopping bags, couples holding hands, and horse-drawn carriages clip-clopping past, as if Charleston were still in the nineteenth century.

Claire's arms were shaking. Her hands were raw from chalk. She felt like she'd been wrung out and then hung up to dry.

The wall had shattered everything she was holding inside, leaving her feeling lighter than she had in months. Now, she sat on the bench with her two best friends, feeling unexpectedly free despite having spent the last twenty minutes crying.

"Well, that was month four," Harper said, smiling. "We're a third of the way through."

"Yeah, but one third of the way to what?" Nina asked.

"I don't know, to whatever we're becoming, I guess."

It was an un-Harper thing to say, almost philo-sophical. The kind of statement she'd normally just deflect with sarcasm.

The horse-drawn carriage turned the corner and disappeared.

"I froze on that wall," Claire said.

"Yep, you did," Nina agreed.

"And I kept going."

"You did that too."

"When's the last time you did that? Kept going when something was hard instead of just trying to make it look easy?" Nina asked.

Nobody answered because the answer was it had been a long time, and everybody knew it.

Claire's phone buzzed.

Greg.

She looked at the screen for a moment, his name staring up at her. She thought about the kitchen, the onions, and your *little club*, and *I just miss you.*

She thought about the way he'd walked back to the den, like the conversation was over when it really hadn't even begun.

She put her phone in her pocket without answering. Harper noticed it. Nina noticed it too, but neither said anything.

"So who picks month five?" Claire asked, because changing the subject was another skill that she had perfected over the years.

"Harper," Nina said. "We're back on track now." Truth be told, they weren't holding tight to the rotation. They would do what was right for each of them to get what they needed from the whole experience.

Harper smiled. She had already decided something. "I have an idea."

"Oh gosh, that smile terrifies me," Claire said.

"Good, because that's rule number one. We're supposed to be a little terrified."

They sat on the bench for a while longer, the three of them, as Charleston moved around them in its beautiful, unhurried way.

Claire's phone buzzed again in her pocket. She let it ring.

On the drive home, alone in her car on the road to Beaufort, she looked at the marsh off in the distance and pulled into a gas station parking lot to open her sketchbook.

The one she'd taken off the shelf after karaoke night and the one that she'd been carrying in her bag for weeks without telling anyone, like her own little secret, just a small rebellion tucked between her wallet and car keys.

She drew the climbing wall, not from the bottom looking up the way that it had terrified her at first, but from the top looking down.

It was a perspective that she'd earned.

It wasn't good. The proportions were way off, and the shading looked clumsy.

It looked like something a talented child might produce, but not like a woman who had once spent entire nights in the College of Charleston art building because she just couldn't stop painting.

But she didn't care.

She tore out the page, put it on the passenger seat, and drove home with the windows down and the radio blaring, the marsh air filling her car.

She didn't check her phone until she pulled into the driveway. Greg had texted twice.

When will you be home?

Then an hour later:

Picking up pizza. What do you want on yours?

She texted back:

I don't care.

Then she folded the drawing, put it in the glove box, and it stayed there hidden and safe, a small piece of who she was becoming tucked inside the car that drove her back and forth between the life she had and the life she was starting to want.

CHAPTER 8

Harper had been to Savannah eleven times in her life, but she had never done anything spontaneous there.

She had gone to Savannah for conferences, mostly, or client dinners, once for a long weekend with Jordan several years ago, where she'd spent half the time answering work emails from the bathroom of her hotel on East Bay Street while he sat on the balcony and read a novel, pretending not to notice.

She had walked the squares and eaten at good restaurants, and she had admired the architecture the way you look at a painting in a museum, from a respectful distance.

Today, she was getting a tattoo.

This was her pick for month five, and she had

chosen it because it was the kind of thing Harper Ellis did not do. You see, Harper Ellis wore silk blouses and expensive heels that cost more than some people's rent.

Harper Ellis signed contracts with a Montblanc pen.

Harper Ellis did not sit in a chair and allow an inked-up stranger to put a needle in her skin. She didn't do permanent things to her body except for the occasional nip or tuck that needed to happen. That was just a necessity.

And this was exactly why she had to do it, because the whole point of this pact was to scare herself, and the thing that scared Harper most was not the pain or the needles, not even the permanence.

It was the loss of control.

It was the idea of marking her body with something she could not take back, could not negotiate, and could not delete from her calendar.

Something permanent from a woman who kept everyone at arm's length so she'd never have to commit to anything she couldn't walk away from.

She kept that particular insight to herself.

They had driven down together, two hours from Beaufort, taking the back roads through the

Lowcountry because Claire said they were prettier, and they were. The Lowcountry was one of the most beautiful places on earth as far as Harper was concerned, and she'd been just about everywhere.

The longer drive was also because they needed the extra time for Nina to talk herself into this, which she eventually did.

The March air, warm through the open windows, carried the decaying smell of the marsh in early spring. It was a smell that was hard to describe to others and very specific to the Lowcountry.

The live oaks along Highway 17 made a tunnel of green and shadow that felt like driving through a cathedral.

"Savannah makes me want to sit on a bench and do nothing for hours," Nina said.

"Yep, that's the Savannah effect," Claire said. "It slows you down whether you want it to or not."

"Well, I suppose I could use some slowing down," Harper said, surprising all three of them, because Harper had never expressed a desire to move at any speed below the maximum in her life.

The parlor was on a side street near Chippewa Square in a narrow brick building with a green door, and it was named Tidewater Ink.

It looked less like a tattoo shop and more like a

bookstore that had changed its mind, which is probably why Harper had chosen it.

She had spent hours reading reviews, comparing portfolios, and even evaluating the cleanliness ratings of seven different tattoo parlors before choosing this one, because even if Harper was being spontaneous, she was going to be thorough about it.

Inside, the walls were exposed brick covered in framed flash art and photographs of finished work. The floors were old hardwood, scuffed but clean. Music played from a speaker behind the counter. It was something acoustic.

The air smelled like clean soap and the faintest trace of cigar smoke from the smoke shop next door. The whole place had a calm, steady energy that felt more like a doctor's office than a den of reckless decisions.

A woman appeared from behind a curtain. She looked like she was probably around forty, with short silver hair and full sleeves of floral tattoos on both arms.

"Harper?" she asked.

"Yes, that's me."

"I'm Wren. We talked on the phone."

She looked at Claire and Nina.

"So is it all three of you?"

"All three of us," Claire said, nervousness obvious in her voice. This wasn't something Claire would've ever suggested.

Wren smiled. She had probably seen this a million times before.

Women of a certain age walking through her door with a mixture of determination and abject terror, about to do something they never thought they would do.

"First tattoos?"

"For me," Claire said. "I've never even had my ears pierced twice."

"I have a little one," Nina said. "A tiny humming-bird on my shoulder blade. David drew it for me." She said it very matter-of-factly, the way she had been saying David's name more and more lately. With love, that didn't sound like she was absolutely drowning.

Harper nodded her head.

"First."

"Okay then," Wren said. "Let's talk about what you all want."

~

They all agreed on matching tattoos, but not on what the matching tattoo should be.

This had been the constant subject of the group chat, spanning two weeks and fifty-three messages.

Claire had suggested they all get a magnolia because, well, she was Claire.

Harper said they needed something geometric and abstract because, well, she was Harper.

Nina said they needed a compass, and they'd almost gone with it until Claire pointed out that a compass implied you were lost, which, while arguably accurate, was not the message she wanted permanently etched on her body.

It was Nina who had finally settled it about three days ago with a text that arrived at almost midnight.

A wave, simple, small, signifies the ocean, signifies the Lowcountry, the way the water keeps moving even when everything else feels still. And then nobody argued with it.

Wren sketched it for them, a tiny, clean wave, no bigger than a quarter, delicate enough to be subtle yet distinct enough to be unmistakable.

She showed them the design on tracing paper, and all three of them leaned over the counter to look at it. Harper felt a tightness in her throat. She didn't entirely understand it. It was just a wave, a tiny drawing of water.

It shouldn't have made her emotional, and yet here she was, standing in a tattoo parlor in Savannah, looking at a drawing the size of a coin and feeling like she was about to do something that mattered so much in a way she simply couldn't articulate.

"Where do you want it?" Wren asked.

Harper didn't hesitate. "Inside of my wrist."

Claire and Nina both looked at her. The wrist was very visible.

The wrist was where clients, colleagues, and even her mother would see it, but Harper was choosing it anyway.

"Ankle," Claire said, "inside and near the bone."

Hidden, of course, because Claire would choose hidden.

Nina wanted to say something, but she stopped and then looked at Wren.

"Can you add initials to mine, like tiny ones next to the wave?"

"Of course, what initials?"

"D-A-V. David Alejandro Vargas."

Wren wrote the letters below the wave on Nina's sketch in a script so small and delicate it looked like the ocean was just whispering his name.

"Perfect," Nina said.

Claire went first because even though she was the most nervous, she believed that going first was just getting it over with. And getting it over with was the way that Claire moved through life without losing her mind.

She sat in the chair with focused intensity, as if undergoing a medical procedure, which was not entirely wrong.

Wren cleaned the spot on her inner ankle, put the stencil on, and picked up the machine. Claire grabbed Nina's hand so hard that Nina actually winced.

"How much have you done?" Claire asked, staring at the ceiling.

"Um, I haven't started yet," Wren said, laughing.

"Oh."

The needle touched her skin, and Claire made a sound like a polite person being electrocuted. She gripped Nina's hand even tighter. Her jaw locked. Her eyes remained on the ceiling as if she were waiting for angels to come down and take her to the clouds.

"Breathe," Wren said calmly.

Claire breathed.

The needle hummed, and Harper watched from the next chair.

Claire Morrison, who organized napkins and baked pound cake and counted to three before speaking to her own husband, was sitting in a chair, allowing a stranger to permanently mark her body.

She was obviously terrified and doing it anyway. It only took about twelve minutes. When Wren finished, she wiped it clean and held up a mirror.

Claire looked at the small wave on her ankle, and a small smile appeared on her face. She was looking at the first thing she had really done for herself in twenty-six years that nobody had asked her to do or needed her to do.

It existed purely because she had chosen it.

"It's so tiny," Claire said.

"It's all yours," Wren said.

Nina went next. She was very calm in the chair, actually calmer than anyone expected. The needle traced the wave, then the initials. Nina watched the whole thing, eyes watching the ink go into her skin.

When Wren finished, Nina ran her thumb gently over the bandage.

"He's going to be on me forever now."

"He was always with you," Harper said. "Now it's just visible on your skin."

Then it was Harper's turn. She sat in the chair. Wren cleaned the inside of her left wrist, the place where her pulse lived, and Harper watched the stencil go on.

She thought about the careful, controlled decisions, every careful, controlled decision she'd made in her last twenty years. The career that she'd built. The apartment with no kitchen table.

The man she'd pushed away because loving him meant needing him, and needing someone was definitely a liability she couldn't afford.

The needle started. It hurt, but not in the way Harper had expected. It was a bit sharp and specific, a focused kind of pain, but Harper found that she actually didn't mind it.

She had spent so long avoiding discomfort of any kind that the honest sting of the needle felt almost like relief. The pain meant that something was happening.

She watched the wave appear on her wrist, small and permanent. When Wren was finished, Harper held her wrist up to the light.

The wave was dark against her clean skin, exactly the small, beautiful thing she would normally never allow herself to have.

She thought about her mother seeing it or her colleagues. She thought about Jordan, who had once told her she was the most closed-off person he'd ever loved.

Now, she thought, *here, there's a crack in the wall, small but real.*

"Are you happy?" Wren asked.

"Yes," Harper said, surprising herself in the process.

The women walked through Savannah afterward, their ankles and wrists bandaged and tender. They felt like they'd gotten away with something. Of course, Savannah had that effect on people. The city felt like a co-conspirator with its hidden gardens and slow pace.

They bought ice cream from a shop on Broughton Street, sat on a bench in Monterey Square, and watched the tourists take photographs of an oak tree from fifteen different angles.

"You know, I just realized," Claire said, licking her cone, "that I'm a fifty-year-old woman sitting on a park bench in Savannah eating ice cream with a fresh tattoo on my ankle. If you had told me this about six months ago, I would have asked you to call a mental health professional."

"Six months ago, you were reorganizing your pantry for fun," Harper said.

"Well, the pantry was very disorganized."

"The pantry was alphabetical, Claire. Then, you organized it by food group."

"Alphabetical was an intermediate step in the process. Food group was supposed to be the final form all along."

Nina was quiet, turning her wrist and looking at the bandage. She hadn't said a whole lot since leaving the parlor.

"So, what are you going to tell Elena?" Claire asked her.

"Nothing. She'll just see it, and she'll have her opinions, and I'll let her have them."

"Elena's opinions could fill an entire stadium."

"Elena's opinions could fill a stadium, a parking lot, and the surrounding neighborhoods." Nina paused. "She'll like that I put the initials, but she'll pretend that she doesn't. She'll say that marking your skin is not how we honor people in her family, and then she'll go home, cry about it in private, and the next time I see her, she'll pretend none of it happened."

"That's a very specific prediction," Harper said, licking her ice cream cone.

"Listen, I've known this woman for years. She's nothing if not consistent."

The sun was starting to drop toward the rooftops, turning the sky a shade of peach that Savannah did better than anywhere else. A horse-drawn carriage clopped past, driven by a man wearing a top hat, who looked like he was genuinely enjoying his job.

The moss swayed in the trees, and the air smelled like jasmine and somehow old brick, if old brick had a smell. There was the faint, salty smell of the river a few blocks away.

Harper looked at her wrist. The bandage was white against her too-pale skin, and beneath it lay something she could never take back. She was surprised to find this feeling didn't produce anxiety, but something more along the lines of peace.

She had marked herself. She had chosen something permanent in a life that she'd built entirely on keeping her options open.

"I need to tell you both something," Harper said.

Claire and Nina looked at her, their ice cream starting to melt, Savannah glowing around them. They waited for Harper to say whatever it was she was about to say.

"I called Jordan back," she said. "Two weeks ago, actually, after the polar plunge."

Claire's ice cream stopped halfway to her mouth. "You did?"

"Yeah, I called him from my car in the parking garage at work. I sat there for twenty minutes first, which I know is ironic because we've been working on Nina's habit of sitting in parking lots, but apparently it's contagious."

"Well, what did he say?" Nina asked.

Harper looked at the square. A couple was walking through it, holding hands, and a child chased a pigeon. It was funny how so many people had their own lives going at the same time, and they were all so different.

"He said, I was hoping you'd call, and then he asked how I was, and I said I was fine. And he said, Harper, how are you, really? You know, nobody ever asks me that. Nobody in my entire life asks me that except you two and maybe this man who builds rocking chairs and still remembers how I take my coffee after four years."

"How do you take your coffee?" Claire asked, as though that was the important detail of this conversation.

"Black with one sugar, which is wrong according to everyone, but Jordan never tried to change it." She paused for a moment. "We talked for forty-five minutes in my car in that parking garage. My assistant texted me three times, and I never answered."

"Wait, you didn't answer James?" Nina said, her eyes wide. "Oh, that is the most romantic thing I've ever heard."

Harper almost smiled, almost. "Anyway, he asked if he could take me to coffee, not dinner, coffee. Because he remembered I don't like first dates. He said this really wasn't a first date, it was a reintroduction."

"A reintroduction," Claire repeated. "Nice."

"That's a good word," Nina said, shrugging her shoulders.

"No, it's a terrifying word. Reintroduction means we're starting over. And starting over means I have to let him see the version of me that exists now, not the version he remembers. And the version that exists now is this fifty-year-old woman who eats toast over her sink and just got a tattoo."

"Did you say yes?" Nina asked.

"To coffee?"

"To the reintroduction?"

"Oh, I said I'd think about it."

"Harper!"

"What? I'm a deliberate person. I like to deliberate."

"You're a scared person, and you stall. I swear,

I've never seen anyone go so out of their way to prevent happiness."

Harper looked at Nina. The directness was new, or maybe old. It was Nina from before when David died, the Nina who would call things out without apology.

"You're right," Harper said. "I am stalling."

"Call him," Claire said. "Say yes."

"It's not that simple."

"You just let a stranger put a permanent mark on your body. You can have coffee with a man who makes rocking chairs."

Harper looked at her wrist again, thinking about the wave beneath the bandage, the small permanent mark she had made because she was trying to learn that not everything in life could be controlled.

"Fine," she said. "I'll call him tonight."

"Tonight," Nina confirmed. "Not tomorrow, not after you've had time to overthink it again and convince yourself it's a bad idea. Tonight."

"You know, you're very bossy for someone who sat in parking lots for months."

"Yeah, well, I'm making up for lost time."

Harper laughed. She sat on that bench with her best friends, ice cream melting down her fingers, a permanent wave on her wrist, and Savannah folding itself into the evening around them.

She thought about Jordan and his workshop in Mount Pleasant, sawdust on his jeans. And she picked up her phone and texted him.

Yes to coffee. You pick the place.

The response came in under a minute.

Tomorrow. Cafe on Vanderhorst, 9:00. I'll be the one who looks like he can't believe his luck.

Harper read it twice.
She didn't show it to Claire or Nina.
She just put her phone back in her pocket and sat there smiling. Claire and Nina looked at each other over Harper's head and said nothing because they knew, and she knew they knew, and that was enough.

~

Claire arrived home at exactly 9:30.

The house was quiet. The den light was on, which meant Greg was in his chair, which meant her world was operating exactly as she had left it. Nothing changed here at her house. It was always the same, day in and day out.

She dropped her bag by the door and went to the kitchen to get a glass of water. Greg appeared in the doorway as he sometimes did, like he was checking on a sound he'd heard from another room.

"So, how was Savannah?" he asked. He was holding a beer and wearing the same khaki shorts he'd been wearing that morning, which was also the same pair he'd been wearing for the last three weekends.

Claire had stopped commenting on it because commenting required energy she no longer had to spend on Greg's wardrobe.

"It was good. Really good, actually."

"What'd you do down there?"

Claire took a breath. She could have lied. She could have said they just walked around, did some shopping, and ate lunch.

She could have made this a small, safe version of herself that Greg was comfortable with, the version that never surprised him, that he didn't have to pay attention to because she never did anything worth paying attention to.

But instead, she sat down on the kitchen stool and pulled up her pant leg. Greg looked at the bandage on her ankle and then at her face.

"What's that? Did you hurt yourself?"

"It's a tattoo."

Greg stared at her. She could see him processing, the gears slowly turning in his brain. Thinking through all the versions of Claire he knew.

Claire, who organized pantries. Claire, who baked pound cake. Claire, who had not surprised him in over two decades. She could see him trying to put the information into the shape of the woman he thought he'd married.

"Have you lost your ever-loving mind?" It was not said with anger. That was the thing about Greg. He never got angry.

He just got confused, which was almost worse because at least anger meant he was paying attention.

Confusion meant she had done something that just didn't compute, something outside the parameters of what he had as Claire stored in his head.

Greg had been an accountant at the same firm for over twenty-five years. His life was simple. Numbers, spreadsheets, recliner, food. That was pretty much it. He didn't love change, and Claire getting a tattoo was a major one.

His first response was not to update his understanding of her, but to question whether there was something wrong with *her*.

Six months ago, Claire would have backtracked. She would have laughed it off, explained it, or made it smaller. She would have said, "Oh, it's just a little thing. Harper talked me into it. It's nothing."

She would have tried to make herself into a version Greg could understand, then filed the real version away in the same place she kept her old sketchbooks and dreams.

But she didn't.

"No," Claire said. "I haven't lost my mind. I got a tattoo. It's an ocean wave. It's small, and I like it."

Greg opened his mouth and then closed it, and then took a sip of beer.

"Well, okay then," he said, and walked back to the den.

Claire sat alone in the kitchen and listened to his recliner engage, and the television come on.

She thought, *That's it? Okay then. I just did the most reckless thing I've done in twenty-six years, and your response is, okay then?"*

She pulled her pant leg down, looked at the kitchen, saw Mason jars, a napkin on the fridge, a gift card she still hadn't used sitting in the junk drawer like a monument to everything her husband didn't understand about her.

Claire went to the guest room. She opened the sketchbook she had started using after karaoke night.

She had four drawings in it now, rough and

unpracticed. She turned to a blank page and drew a small, simple, and permanent wave.

Then she drew another and another and another. The page filled up with waves, each one slightly different.

She sat there drawing until midnight, alone in the guest room of the house she had shared with this man for two decades, almost three.

The only sound was the pencil on the paper and the television through the wall, and the quiet, ever-growing knowledge that something was going to have to change.

CHAPTER 9

The idea was Asheville, North Carolina. It was Harper's pick. It was month six, the halfway point of the pact. Not a single event like karaoke or the plunge or the tattoos, but something a little bigger.

Two days on the road, away from everything, away from Greg's recliner and Harper's corner office and Nina's quiet little house on Edisto.

Two days of being nobody's wife, nobody's boss, and nobody's grieving widow. Just three women in a car with a playlist and no particular obligations.

It didn't seem like a scary thing to do, at least to other people. But to Harper, leaving work without taking her computer was a big deal. She had never been one who relaxed easily, and this trip was a challenge for her.

Then there was Nina, who hadn't been away from home overnight since David died. She had told herself this was because of Lucia, because a sixteen-year-old shouldn't be left alone, which, of course, was a reasonable concern, but it completely ignored the fact that Elena lived ten minutes away and had been volunteering to take Lucia for a weekend since the funeral happened.

The real reason Nina hadn't gone anywhere was actually pretty simple and probably harder to admit. Leaving the house meant leaving the last place David had lived.

His boots by the door, his grungy old robe hanging on the hook, the dent in his side of the mattress that she still didn't have the heart to flip over.

Going away felt like leaving him behind, even though she knew in the logical part of her brain that grief hadn't managed to suffocate, that David was not in those boots or the robe or the mattress. He was gone, and those things were simply just *things*.

But his things were all she had left, and letting go of them for even two days felt like stepping off a ledge.

She packed her bags anyway.

She actually packed, unpacked, and repacked it a

couple more times because the first time she packed it, she did it like she was leaving for a month.

And the second time, she packed like she was going to the grocery store. Finally, on the third try, she packed like a normal human going on a two-day road trip.

Lucia watched her from the doorway of her bedroom with her arms crossed and one eyebrow raised.

"You're packing a sweater for Asheville in April," Lucia said.

"Well, the mountains can be cool at nighttime."

"It's going to be seventy degrees."

"I like to be prepared."

"Okay, you packed four pairs of socks for two days. That's not being prepared. That's being anxious."

Nina looked at the socks. She put two pairs back. "Fine. Happy?"

"Delighted." Lucia uncrossed her arms. "Mom, you're going to have fun. You remember fun, right? That's the thing that happens when you're not watching HGTV and pretending you're fine."

"But I like HGTV."

"Nobody likes HGTV that much. You just watch it so the house isn't so quiet."

Nina's hands froze on the zipper. Sometimes

Lucia said things like this, things that were precisely and surgically accurate. Nina wondered when her daughter had become the most perceptive person she knew.

Sixteen years old, and she could see through every wall Nina built.

"I'll be fine at Abuela's," Lucia said. "She's making tamales, and we're going to watch telenovelas. I will be completely supervised and definitely overfed. Go."

"I love you," Nina said.

"I know. Bring me something weird from a gas station."

Claire picked her up at eight o'clock.

Harper was already in the passenger seat with her sunglasses on, expensive coffee in hand, looking like a woman in a car commercial, except they were in Claire's twelve-year-old Honda Pilot with a dent in the passenger door and a backseat that smelled of art supplies Claire had started accumulating over the past three months.

There were colored pencils in the center console, a sketchbook under the driver's seat, and evidence of this woman who was quietly and carefully allowing herself to want things again.

Nina climbed into the backseat, and they pulled out of her crushed shell driveway. The marsh fell away behind them as they crossed the bridge off Edisto.

The drive to Asheville was five hours, give or take, depending on how many times Claire stopped at a gas station for coffee or how many times Harper demanded they skip the scenic route in favor of the interstate.

They compromised, interstate to Columbia, then Highway 26 through the foothills, where the land-scape shifted from the flat Lowcountry to rolling Piedmont to the blue ridges of the mountains.

The air changed from the salt and pluff mud to pine and earth. Of course, their conversations in the car were the best part. Not the arrival or the destina-tion, but the hours in between where the three of them were sealed in a small space with nowhere to go and nothing to do but talk.

They'd always been *very* good at this.

Even in college, long drives to the beach or road trips to football games, or that three-hour crawl from Charleston to Atlanta for Harper's first job interview.

Those car conversations had shaped them and

were where real things got said. Admissions they would make to each other and then deny if it was ever brought up again.

"I have a confession," Claire said, somewhere past Columbia.

"You're secretly a morning person?" Harper said.

"I'm already a morning person."

"Nobody should enjoy mornings as much as you do."

"Anyway, my confession," Claire said, rolling her eyes, "is that I've been sleeping in the guest room."

The car went quiet.

"Since when?" Nina asked.

"Since the tattoo, so a little over three weeks."

"Does Greg realize this?" Harper asked.

"Uh, yes, Greg knows I'm sleeping in the guest room. I am missing from our bed, after all. He just hasn't asked why." Claire's hands were steady on the wheel. "He hasn't asked. Three weeks, and he hasn't even asked me why I moved out of our bedroom."

Nina leaned forward from the backseat. She could see the set of Claire's jaw and the small line between her brows.

She thought about David, who would have followed her into the guest room within five minutes, wearing a confused expression and asking

dozens of questions, because David noticed everything and cared about everything.

He would not have shared a house with a woman
he loved without knowing why she'd moved into a
different room.

But David was David, and Greg was most definitely Greg. Comparing the two wasn't fair, but
Nina thought about it anyway. She suspected Claire
had thought it, too.

"What do you want to happen?" Nina asked.

"I don't know. That's my honest answer. I keep
waiting to know, and I just don't. I don't want to
leave right now. I don't want things to stay this way
either. I don't know what's in between those two
things. I just know we can't keep living like this."

"Counseling," Harper said, not as a suggestion,
more like a label. "I mean, that's what's in between."

"Greg won't go to counseling. I've brought it up
twice over the last few years. He says we're fine."

"You're sleeping in separate rooms."

"He'll say it's because I'm going through a phase
or something equally ridiculous. I don't know.
Maybe I am going through a phase."

Harper made a sound close to the one she made
in board meetings when someone said something so
wrong it didn't even deserve a response.

"It's not a phase," Claire said quietly, being honest

with them and herself. "I am the most awake I've been in over twenty years. That's not a phase. That's a wake-up call."

The pines thickened before them. The mountains appeared in the distance, blue and layered, getting closer.

"You don't have to decide anything right now," Nina said. "You just have to keep being honest with yourself and with us, even with Greg if he'll listen."

"And what if he won't?"

"Well, then you'll know something from that, too. Life is about data. Facts. You make decisions when you have enough of both. You'll know when you know," Harper said in her most business-like voice.

Claire nodded.

She didn't say anything else for a few miles, and Nina let the silence hold them as the mountains got closer.

They stopped for lunch at a little diner outside Hendersonville that looked like it hadn't changed one bit since 1974.

Wood paneling, vinyl booths that had seen better days, a jukebox in the corner that worked, playing a Dolly Parton song at a volume that suggested the owner believed Dolly deserved to be heard by the entire building and possibly the county.

The menu was laminated and included a section titled "Juanita's Favorites," which they assumed referred to the owner and turned out to refer to the cook, a woman in her 70s who came out of the kitchen to personally deliver their fried chicken and ask where they were from.

"The Lowcountry," Claire said.

"All three of you?" Juanita looked them over.

"College friends," Nina said. "We've known each other for thirty years."

"Thirty years?" Juanita shook her head. "You know what keeps friendship alive that long?"

"What?" Harper asked.

"Minding your business when you need to and not minding it when you shouldn't." She put down a basket of biscuits that hadn't been asked for. "You're on a trip?"

"Yeah, road trip," Claire said. "Asheville."

"What for?"

The three of them looked at each other. The answer was complicated.

A napkin, a pact, twelve adventures, a dead husband, a dying marriage, a man who built rocking chairs, a fifty-year-old woman who had just started drawing again after twenty-seven years.

The answer was an entire book in and of itself.

"We made a deal to do one scary thing a month for a year," Nina said. "This month is a road trip."

Juanita looked at them. She let out a big belly laugh that filled the whole diner.

"Honey, that's the best thing I've heard all week. I'm seventy-three and still try to do one scary thing a month. Last month, I went on a date with a man from my church. First date in eleven years."

"Well, how was it?" Harper asked.

"Terrible. That man talked about his prostate for forty-five minutes, but I got through it. The next one will be better, or maybe it won't, but at least I'm in the game." She tapped the table twice. "Y'all eat. Biscuits are on the house. Anybody doing what you're doing deserves free biscuits."

She disappeared into the kitchen, and the three of them just sat at the vinyl booth eating fried chicken and biscuits that were, Nina had to admit, some of the best she'd ever had.

Dolly sang loudly from the jukebox about working nine to five, and the afternoon sun came through the window in a piercing beam.

"I want to be Juanita when I grow up," Claire said.

"Oh, Juanita would eat Greg alive," Harper said, laughing.

"Juanita would eat all of us alive."

Asheville was everything the Lowcountry wasn't.

Mountains instead of marshes, cool air instead of thick, choking heat, streets that went up instead of being flat in every direction. The city sat in a valley, surrounded by big blue ridges, and it had the energy of a place that drew artists, musicians, and people who had decided at some point that the conventional path in life just wasn't for them.

Nina loved it immediately.

They checked into a small hotel near the Grove Arcade, a room with two beds and a pullout couch, which Claire insisted she would take because she always took the worst option in any given situation. Harper pointed out this was both generous and slightly masochistic.

They walked and walked. That was the adventure, really. Not any single thing, but the accumulated hours of walking through a city none of them knew, going into shops and galleries, sitting on benches outside the bookstore, eating chocolate, watching street musicians play for tips on the corner of Lexington and Broadway.

Harper bought a scarf she didn't need from a woman selling handmade goods on the sidewalk. The woman had a hairless cat named Peppy and no teeth in her mouth.

Claire sketched in her notebook while they waited for a table at a restaurant Nina had found on her phone, a small place that had a patio overlooking the mountains.

Nina tried on a hat in a vintage shop and looked at herself in the mirror. She saw, for the first time in a long time, a woman who looked like she might be having a good day.

Dinner was on the patio. The mountains went purple as the sun dropped, and the air cooled enough that she needed that sweater Lucia had told her not to pack. The food was good, the wine was better, and the conversation turned the way it always did when they were on their second glass, honest and unguarded.

"Harper update," Claire said. "We need the Jordan report."

"There is no Jordan report."

"But you had coffee with him three weeks ago. There's got to be a report."

Harper rearranged her silverware. She did this when she was stalling.

"We've had coffee twice," she said.

Claire set her wine glass down, and Nina stopped chewing.

"Twice?" Nina said.

"The first time was the whole reintroduction, and the second time was because I'd already gone to the trouble of finding a parking spot on Vanderhorst Street, and parking in Charleston is its own form of torture."

"Well, what was it like?" Nina asked.

Harper was quiet for a moment. The candle flickered on the table between them.

"He looks the same," she said. "Older, a little more gray, still has the sawdust thing going on, like he just walked out of his workshop five minutes before he showed up. He ordered black coffee and remembered I take mine with one sugar. He didn't bring up the past, not once. He just asked me what I'd been doing for four years and then listened like he cared."

"Because he does care," Claire said. "That man has always adored you."

"I know. That's what scares me. I spent four years convincing myself I was better off alone. Then this man shows up with his sawdust and patience and his one sugar, and I have to reconsider everything."

"You mean reconsider that you're fine alone? Or that alone is the same as fine?"

Nobody rushed to fill the pause. The waiter came and went. The mountains disappeared into the dark.

"I told him about the pact," Harper said. "He wanted to see the tattoo."

"What did he say?"

"He looked at it for a long time, and then he said, 'That's cool.' And he smiled, and it was the same smile I remembered. I had to leave because I was about to do something completely out of character."

"Like what?" Claire asked.

"Like stay."

Nina felt the weight of the words settle.

Stay.

Such a small word for such a terrifying act.

Harper, who left. Harper, who kept her options open. Harper, who had a beautiful apartment with no kitchen table, because a kitchen table implied someone else would sit with her there.

For Harper, staying was the bravest thing she could do.

"Well, then stay next time," Nina said. Harper looked at her. "I mean it. The next time you're sitting across from him, and you wanna leave because things are getting real, just don't. Stay. See what happens."

"What if what happens is that I fall for him all

over again, and then it doesn't work out, and I end up feeling worse than before?"

"Well, what if it does work?"

Harper didn't answer.

Getting to the hotel room at midnight was the best part of the whole trip.

Claire decided to sleep on the pullout couch with her sketchbook beside her so she could draw the view of the restaurant patio from memory. Harper was on one of the beds, wearing the plush hotel bathrobe, texting someone she refused to identify, but it was obviously Jordan, based on how she kept angling her phone away from everyone. Nina was on the other bed, propped up against the headboard.

For the first time in a year and a half, she wasn't thinking about going home.

This was the thing she'd been the most afraid of. Not the trip, not even the distance, not even leaving Lucia with Elena. She'd been afraid that she would get here and want to stay, that she would find out there was a version of her that existed beyond her little cottage on Edisto and David's boots by the door, that there might be a version of her that still wanted things, that wanted to eat dinner on a patio watching mountains go purple, that wanted to walk through a city she didn't know, that wanted to lie on a hotel bed at midnight listening to her best friends talk instead of sitting in her home and suffocating from the fog of grief.

She wanted *tomorrow*, and that was new.

For almost two years, tomorrow had been something she just had to get through. It had been a series of hours between waking up on the wrong side of the bed and falling back asleep.

Now she was lying in a hotel in Asheville with her two best friends, and she actually wanted to know what came next. She wanted to wake up and eat breakfast at a place they hadn't found yet and walk down a street she'd never seen. She wanted to be alive, not just surviving, but alive.

The feeling was so unfamiliar to her that it took a moment to name it. It sat on her chest like a bird that had been in a cage so long, it didn't trust what to do with an open door.

Anticipation. That's what it was. She was looking forward to something.

"Nina?" Claire said from the pullout sofa. She was lying on her stomach with her sketchbook open, a pencil in her hand, and looked like she was back in middle school. "You're smiling."

"Am I?"

"Yeah, you're lying there smiling at the ceiling like it told you a joke."

"I guess I'm just… well, I'm happy," she said it carefully, testing the word to see if it felt right. "I think I'm happy right now."

Claire stopped drawing. Harper looked up from her phone.

"Yeah?" Claire said.

"Yeah." Nina kept her eyes on the ceiling. "It actually feels a little different than I remembered. It's not a big loud thing. It's just this, lying here, being with you two, knowing there's a tomorrow that I'm actually looking forward to."

Claire put her pencil down. Harper put her phone down. Nobody said anything for a moment.

"David would be so glad," Claire said. "He would be so, so glad."

"He would be jealous," Nina said. "You know he always wanted to go to Asheville. He had a whole list of restaurants, and he kept adding to it. I think that list is still on the fridge at home under that palm tree magnet."

"Well, we should go to one of his restaurants tomorrow," Harper said.

Nina looked at her. "Really?"

"Pick the one he wanted to go to most. We'll have lunch there."

Nina picked up her phone and scrolled until she found the photo she had taken months ago of his list, still pinned to her fridge, his handwriting slanting upward.

There were seven restaurants.

He'd circled one of them twice and drawn a star next to it, some barbecue place on the south side.

"This one," she said, holding up the phone.

"Well, then that's where we're going," Claire said.

Nina put her phone on the nightstand. She pulled the covers up. She listened to Claire's pencil scratching and Harper's phone buzzing with a man's texts that she was trying to learn to let back in.

Outside the hotel window, Asheville hummed, and the mountains stood in the dark, waiting, patient. And nobody knew that a woman in Room 214 was looking forward to tomorrow for the first time in a long time.

Nina closed her eyes. She didn't dream about David or that awful day he left.

She dreamed about a road she hadn't driven yet, stretching out ahead of her. She slept through the night, *the whole night.*

No waking up at 3 a.m. to reach for a body that wasn't there. No staring at the ceiling fan. No lying on the wrong side of the bed.

When she woke up, the mountains were pink

with sunrise, and Claire was already dressed. She was holding three coffees somehow, and Harper was pretending that she hadn't been up since 6 a.m., texting Jordan.

And Nina thought, *Yes, I want more of this.*

She got dressed and drank her coffee. She told Claire about the barbecue place, and they checked out of the hotel and got into the car.

The drive home later today was five hours long, and Nina was in absolutely no rush to get there.

Yes, it was crazy that they had come just to stay one night, but they would spend the whole day meandering around Asheville before hitting the road home. And even though it was stressful and crazy, she was thankful to be doing it all with her best friends.

CHAPTER 10

Claire was wearing lipstick for the first time in years. She wasn't really sure how she felt about it.

She'd bought the lipstick at a drugstore in Beaufort on Tuesday, standing in the cosmetic aisle for eleven whole minutes trying to choose a color. It was called Rosewood, which she thought sounded elegant and literary, but it made her lips look like she'd had injections.

This lipstick was for speed dating.

This was Nina's pick for month seven.

Nina, who six months ago couldn't even walk into a grocery store without sitting in the parking lot for twenty minutes, had signed the three of them up for speed dating at a wine bar in downtown Charleston.

When she texted the group chat with the plan, Harper responded with a single word:

Why?

It wasn't even a question. It was a statement of disgust.

Claire had responded with,

I'm a married woman.

It wasn't a great marriage right now, but she had the certificate.

And Nina had responded with,

I know, but that's not the point. The point is sitting across from a stranger and being interesting. When was the last time any of us had to be interesting?

Claire didn't have an answer for that because the honest answer was really embarrassing.

The last time she'd been interesting to a stranger was so long ago she couldn't even remember it. The last time she'd been interesting to her own husband was even longer ago.

She was a third-grade teacher who organized

pantries, baked pound cake, and slept in the guest room of a marriage that had gone so quiet you could hear the refrigerator hum.

She looked at herself in the bathroom mirror, her in her Rosewood lipstick.

She'd chosen a green blouse that she bought last week, and she never would have chosen it six months ago because it was way too bright and noticeable.

Her hair was down. She was even wearing earrings.

Greg was in the den, of course. It was hard to tell the den and Greg apart these days. Greg was more married to the den than to her. She could hear the television through the wall, the murmur of a game or a show or whatever it was he had retreated into tonight.

She had told him she was going out with Nina and Harper, and he'd said, "Have fun."

Two words.

The same two words he said every time she left the house now, delivered with the same flatness, as if she were a neighbor he was being polite to rather than a wife he was losing.

She hadn't told him about speed dating. She told herself it was because he wouldn't understand, which was completely and totally true.

But the deeper truth was that she didn't want to see his face when she said it.

She didn't want to watch him process the information that his wife of two decades was sitting across from another man, not because she wanted another man, but because she wanted to remember what it felt like to be *seen*.

Greg would hear the term "speed dating" and just assume she was looking for a replacement.

She absolutely wasn't. She was looking for a mirror.

She wanted to sit across from someone and see them recognize her worth in four minutes of attention. She wanted someone to ask her questions and really listen to her answers.

She put the lipstick in her purse, turned off the bathroom light, and left.

The wine bar was on East Bay Street. That was Harper's territory. So Harper was already there, sitting at the bar, drinking a glass of something that was expensive, obviously.

"There are name tags," she said instead of greeting them. "They want us to wear them."

"Well, that's kind of how speed dating works,"

Claire replied. "These are strangers who don't know our names."

"I'm the vice president of a major financial firm. I don't wear name tags. If I wanted to wear a name tag, I'd be a mechanic or a refrigerator repairman."

"Well, you wore a name tag at the tattoo parlor."

"That was a sticker Wren put on me as a joke. I didn't even notice until we were in the car."

Nina arrived looking like a totally different person. It was like watching an old photograph slowly develop.

She was wearing a dark red dress that Claire had never even seen. Her hair was loose around her shoulders, and she wore a necklace that caught the light as she moved.

She looked kind of like Nina from before, but not exactly. She looked like a new, upgraded version, one that had the same history but operated differently. Kind of like when you upgrade your computer's operating system. You still have the same computer, but it works in a completely different way, with entirely new features.

"You look great," Claire said.

"Oh, thank you. It's Lucia's dress. Trust me, she supervised my entire outfit. She said I was basically a presentation. In fact, she did a presentation. She actually had slides."

"Slides?" Harper said, laughing.

"Yes, on her phone. She showed me three different options and then ranked them by sophistication and approachability. She's sixteen, but I have absolutely no idea where she gets this."

"David," Claire and Harper said at the same time.

Nina smiled. There was only a little bit of sadness behind the smile. Most of it was just easy.

The event coordinator was a woman named Bev, with the energy of a summer camp counselor and the organizational skills of a general.

She pulled together thirty or so people in the back room of the wine bar, where the small tables had been set up in rows of two chairs each. There were candles lit and wine glasses waiting.

There were roughly the same number of men and women, and all of them seemed to be somewhere around forty-five to sixty years old. Everybody had that same expression on their face, a sort of hopeful dread.

Claire imagined that she was probably wearing that same expression too, although she wasn't going to take a chance and look in the mirror.

"Okay, everybody," Bev announced, clapping her hands with excitement. "You have four minutes at each table. When you hear the bell, the men will rotate. Women, just stay seated. At the end of the night, you can write who you're interested in on the cards I've given you. If there's a match, we'll put you in touch with each other. Now, the most important rule is that everybody has fun. Remember, this is supposed to be fun. This is not a tax audit."

"This does *not* feel fun," Harper murmured.

"It feels like I'm going in for a big performance review," Claire said.

"Oh, good Lord, it's four minutes," Nina said. "We can survive anything for four minutes. We survived thirty seconds in the Atlantic in the bitter cold."

"Well, the Atlantic didn't ask me what I do for a living," Harper said, crossing her arms. "Or make me wear a name tag."

The bell rang, and speed dating began.

Claire's first date, which sounded really weird given that she was married and had no interest in dating anyone, was named Tom.

He sold insurance.

And he smiled too much.

And he had those big, overly white, capped teeth that made him look like he might have been a horse in a previous life.

He asked her what she did for a living. She said

she was a third-grade teacher. His response was, "Oh, that must be very rewarding."

She said it was. She wasn't sure if she meant it. It depended on the day you asked.

He asked her if she had any kids of her own. She said two, grown.

He asked if she was divorced. And she said no, she was married.

His smile flickered for a moment. She could see him recalculating something in his head.

And then he spent the remaining two minutes just telling her about his boat.

She zoned out.

Her second date was a man named Phil. He was recently widowed and talked about his late wife for three of the four minutes. It was gentle and loving. And Claire listened.

She thought of Nina and wanted to reach across the table and hold his hand. But she didn't, because that wasn't what this was supposed to be.

And then she thought about Greg and wondered if, after she died, would he talk about her for three minutes straight at a speed date?

She doubted it.

He would probably talk about the Braves.

Her third date was a woman who had acciden-tally ended up at the wrong table. She was looking for a trivia night that was happening in the front room. Claire pointed her in the right direction. They both laughed. And it was the most natural conversation she had all evening.

Claire loved trivia. She almost followed the woman into the other room.

Her fourth date was a man named Richard. He was a retired English professor.

He did have kind eyes and a nice sport coat with those cool patches on the elbows, but he also had that particular quality of attention that comes from spending decades listening to students talk about what they think a poem means.

He asked Claire what she liked to do. She opened her mouth to say what she always said: cooking, reading, and spending time with her family. You know, the menu of acceptable answers that you carry around.

She had done that for twenty-six years, the resume of a woman who had defined herself entirely by her relationship with other people.

Instead, she suddenly said, "I've started drawing again. I used to paint in college, and I stopped, and I just started drawing again a few months ago."

He leaned forward, as if he were actually interested.

"What do you draw?"

"Waves mostly, the marsh, my friends some-times." She paused. "I'm not very good yet. I guess I'm relearning."

"Well, relearning is the most interesting part of it," he said. "It means you already know something, but now you're choosing to know it differently."

The bell rang. Richard smiled, tapped the table, and moved on.

Claire sat there for a moment, looking at the empty chair across from her.

She didn't want Richard. She didn't want Tom or Phil or any of the men who had rotated around her table for over an hour. She didn't want someone new.

What she wanted was to sit across from some-one, anyone, and say, "I've started drawing again." And have that person lean forward, as Richard did, instead of shrugging, as Greg would likely do.

The problem wasn't that she needed a different man.

The problem was that her own husband would have said, "Oh, that's nice," and then changed the subject.

But Richard, a total stranger, had leaned in.

That was the gap in her life. It was the whole thing. She didn't want an affair. She didn't want to have a crush on someone. She wasn't someone who was going to take the avenue of betrayal.

She just now had the devastating clarity of realizing that a stranger in a sport coat with those cool elbow patches had shown more interest in her inner life in four minutes than Greg had shown in the last four years.

~

Harper was having a very different kind of night.

Claire could see her from across the room, about three tables away, sitting with her rigid posture, as if she were being questioned by the FBI under a bright light.

Most of her dates lasted the whole four minutes only because the bell hadn't rung yet.

She was polite. She was efficient, as always. She was treating each conversation like an interview, which was exactly what she'd said it felt like and exactly how Harper handled it.

This is how she handled anything she couldn't control: by controlling it so thoroughly that no actual connection could ever sneak through.

On her sixth or seventh rotation, something changed.

Claire noticed it because she was pretending to listen to this man named Gary, who was talking about his timeshare in Hilton Head, but she was actually watching Harper out of the corner of her eye.

She had no interest in Gary's timeshare.

Harper was laughing. It wasn't the performative laugh that she normally used. It was a real laugh. She threw her head back slightly. Claire had heard it maybe a dozen times in the past year.

The man across from her was in his mid-fifties, wearing wire-rimmed glasses. He had a stillness about him. He was talking, and Harper was actually listening.

She wasn't even checking her phone, which was one of the most astonishing things Claire had seen all evening.

The bell rang.

The man stood up and said something that made Harper smile, and then moved to the next table.

Harper watched him go. She picked up her wine glass, took a long drink, and then Claire could read the expression on her face because she'd been reading Harper's expressions for thirty years.

She had just been surprised by something she hadn't expected. And she was probably trying to make a case in her brain of why she should totally ignore it.

Later, in the bathroom between the rounds, Claire cornered her.

"Who was that?"

"Who was who?"

"The man with the glasses, the one who was making you laugh and kind of throw your head back."

"His name is Peter. He teaches history at the Citadel. And he was very pleasant."

"Again, you threw your head back."

"I did not throw my head back."

"Harper, I was watching you. You threw your head back. And you laughed. You almost gave yourself whiplash. You don't do that for someone who's just pleasant."

Harper reapplied her very red lipstick. "He was funny. He told a joke about the Citadel's admission process that was actually pretty clever. And I appreciate the construction of good humor. That's all."

"Are you going to check his name on the card to indicate interest, as Bev said?"

"I'm seeing Jordan."

"You've had coffee with Jordan two times. That's not seeing someone."

"Well, it's the beginning of seeing someone. It's

like the preamble of seeing. I'm in the opening chapters of seeing."

"What about Peter?"

She capped her lipstick. "Peter is irrelevant. Peter is a little speed-dating story I'll tell at parties. He's a man I spoke to for four minutes in a wine bar, and I will never speak to him again."

She said it with such finality that Claire had to let it go because pushing Harper was like trying to push a boulder uphill with a teaspoon.

But still, she filed it away.

Not because she thought Harper should pursue Peter necessarily, but because Peter proved something Harper actually needed to see.

That she was capable of laughing with a stranger, of being surprised, of letting her guard down for a whole four minutes.

If she could do that with Peter, then she could do it with Jordan. The muscle still worked. She just needed to strengthen it.

Nina's night was the quietest of the three.

Claire didn't find out until afterward, in the parking lot, when they all stood by Claire's car in the warm May air and debriefed. They debriefed the way they always did, thoroughly and honestly, with the wine still warm in their systems and plenty of humor.

"I met someone," Nina said, leaning against the car.

She said it like it was important, but without any buildup, as if she had just told them a tornado was heading their way.

Claire and Harper stood there, frozen.

"His name is Sam," Nina said. "He's a landscape architect who lives on James Island. He lost his wife to breast cancer two years ago." She was looking at the ground, at her shoes, actually, at anything but their faces. "He was very kind, didn't try too hard, asked me all about Edisto, and I told him about the marsh. He told me about the garden he designed for the hospice center where his wife was. We just talked. It wasn't a romantic thing. It wasn't anything, really, I guess. But when the bell rang, I didn't want him to leave the table. That hasn't happened to me since David."

The parking lot was quiet. A car passed. Somewhere in the bar, they were playing music that leaked through the walls.

"That's great, Nina," Claire said.

"Is it? Because I feel super guilty. Like, I feel as though I just betrayed David by enjoying a four-minute conversation with a man who designs gardens."

"You didn't betray anyone," Harper said. "David wouldn't consider a conversation a betrayal. He would consider it a new beginning for you."

"I know that in my head. I really do. My head is very reasonable about all this. I have a very reasonable head, but my heart is less cooperative."

"So did you check his name on the card?" Claire asked.

Nina was quiet for a moment.

"Yes."

Claire reached over and squeezed her arm.

Harper made a squeal that sounded like delight, which she quickly converted into a cough.

"Let's not make it a thing," Nina said, pleadingly.

"We would never," Harper responded.

"Oh, it's already a thing," Claire said.

"It is not a thing. It's just a card with a little name written on it, and I checked the little box at a speed dating event, of all things, for a man I spoke to for about four minutes. That is the whole thing, and it is definitely not a thing."

"It's a little bit of a thing," Harper said, holding up her thumb and forefinger.

Nina looked at them, the two women leaning against the car, grinning at her. She shook her head and smiled. It was an embarrassed, hopeful, scared smile.

"If he calls, I'll have coffee with him, but that's it. Coffee, in a public place during daylight hours. Plus, maybe he didn't write my name down. That's entirely possible."

"Those are reasonable terms, but you are acting like he's an axe murderer," Harper said. "Anyway, I approve."

"I wasn't asking for approval."

"Well, you have it anyway."

They got into the car. Claire drove with the windows down and the salt air coming off the harbor. They crossed over the bridge in Charleston, lights spreading out behind them.

Nina was quiet in the backseat, and Harper was quiet in the front.

Claire drove through the dark toward Beaufort, thinking about Richard and his sport coat and his elbow patches and his forward-leaning. She would've never thought someone leaning forward was so important to her.

And then she thought about Greg and his recliner. His backward leaning. His "have fun." She thought about the gap between those two responses and what it meant about the life she built.

She got home at midnight. The house was dark.

Greg was snoring. The porch light was off again. He didn't even leave it on to make sure she got in okay.

Claire stood in the kitchen. She stared at the napkin on the fridge. She looked at the junk drawer where the gift card still sat.

She looked at the dark hallway leading to their bedroom, where her husband would definitely be sleeping on his side, facing the wall.

She went to the guest room and opened her sketchbook. She drew a woman sitting across the table from a stranger.

He was leaning forward.

She didn't draw the stranger's face. She only drew her own.

The fight started over chicken. Chicken. Can you even imagine such a thing?

Claire had made roasted chicken for dinner. This was not an unusual thing. She made roasted chicken at least once a week because Greg liked it and it was easy.

She'd been cooking dinner for the same man for well over two decades, and at some point, the meals had stopped being choices and had become rotations.

Roasted chicken was on Tuesday, the way spaghetti was on Thursday, the way leftovers were on Sunday. Pizza from their favorite place was sprinkled in between.

She had seasoned it just the way she always did,

with rosemary and lemon and a little too much garlic, because she loved garlic. Greg tolerated garlic.

She set it on the table for two with the everyday plates and the everyday napkins. She put the salt and pepper shakers that were shaped like little lighthouses that they bought on their honeymoon in Maine twenty-six years ago, back when they bought things together, back when a lighthouse seemed charming instead of ironic. Now, even a lighthouse couldn't help her see the way home to her marriage that she used to love.

Greg came to the table. He sat down, and he looked at the chicken as if someone was about to walk him straight down to the electric chair.

"Chicken again?"

Claire counted to three. *One, two, three.*

"Yes. Is that a problem?"

"Well, no. I just feel like we eat chicken a lot."

"We do eat chicken a lot. You like chicken."

"I suppose I like chicken fine. I'm just saying we could mix it up a little bit."

Claire sat down across from him. She picked up her fork, but then put it down. Then she picked it up again. The lighthouse salt shaker stared at her from the middle of the table, and she thought about how many meals she had eaten at this table, in this same kitchen, across from this same man. Thousands. Literally thousands of meals that she had cooked, every single one of them. And never once in the twenty-six years she had cooked had he offered to cook instead.

"What would you like me to make?" She kept her voice steady. Her hands under the table were not.

"I don't know. Something different."

"Like what?"

"I don't know, Claire. I'm not a cook."

She counted to three again. She'd been counting to three in her marriage for so long that she did it quickly now. There were no pauses. She held a tiny breath that nobody ever noticed, not even her most of the time. Right now, she noticed it. She noticed her jaw tightening, her shoulders rising to her earlobes, the way she braced her body every single time. She was swallowing words that she really wanted to say, and she had just grown tired of swallowing.

"You could cook," she said matter-of-factly.

He looked up from his plate. He looked as if he'd just been told something in a language he didn't speak. He was confused, maybe offended, uncertain how to respond.

"Excuse me, what?"

"If you want something different, you are able to cook it yourself. The kitchen is right there," she said, pointing across the room. "It's been right there for twenty-six years."

Greg set his fork down. He wasn't even angry. It was like he was doing it carefully, the way you would set down a tool so you didn't accidentally cut off your hand. Or you'd set down a bag of steaks when an angry bear approaches.

"What is going on with you?"

"Nothing is going on with me."

"Oh, something's going on. You've been acting weird for months. You're gone all the time. You got a tattoo. You sleep in the guest room. And now you're picking a fight over chicken."

"I am not picking a fight. I am just suggesting that you could participate in the feeding of yourself."

"See, that right there," Greg pointed at her. "That tone. You never used to talk to me like that."

Claire felt something rising up in her chest like lava. She recognized it as the thing she'd been counting to three to avoid. Not anger, exactly, but something bigger than that. What was bigger than anger? Something that had been sitting in the basement of her marriage for so long, it felt like it had grown roots.

"You're right," she said. "I didn't used to talk to

you like that. I used to count to three and then say something nice. I've been counting to three and saying nice things since the millennium, Greg. Do you know how many times I've counted to three in this marriage?"

He stared at her. "What are you talking about?"

"I'm talking about the fact that I've spent all of our marriage making everything in this house work. The cooking, the cleaning, the kids' school, the holidays, the birthday parties, thank-you notes, groceries, appointments, all of it. Every single piece of life I've managed. And you've sat in that den, put an indentation in a ratty old recliner from your butt cheeks, and watched the Braves, assuming that everything would just keep happening."

The kitchen went quiet. She could hear the refrigerator humming. She could feel the napkin hanging on the fridge, as if it were watching her, a witness. How had this all started with a napkin?

"I work too, Claire," Greg said. His voice had gone careful, like he was navigating land he had never been to. "I've worked this whole time. I've provided for this family."

"Yes, you have. You've worked, and you've provided. You've been a good father and a reliable human. I'm not saying you haven't done those things."

"Then what are you saying?"

She looked at him, the man she'd been married to. He had been steady and kind, making her feel safe when she was twenty-four years old. He'd held her hand in the delivery room twice. He had built a bookshelf for their daughter's room and mowed the lawn every Saturday. He'd paid the mortgage on time every month for all twenty-six years. He was not a bad man. He was not a cruel man. He was a man who had done everything he'd been taught that a husband should do and just could not understand why that wasn't enough.

"I'm saying that you gave me a gift card for my fiftieth birthday."

He blinked. "What?"

"You gave me a gift card. Not even one to a specific store that you know I like, a universal one that I could use at the gas station, the grocery store, or to buy adult diapers. You couldn't be bothered to choose a store, Greg. I turned fifty, and you gave me a piece of plastic that said, 'Hey, here's something worth thirty dollars at any participating retailer,' and you thought that was fine."

"You said you liked it."

"I say I like everything! That's what I do to survive. I say I like things. I say I'm fine. I say, 'Oh, no big deal.' I've been saying that for so long that you actually believe me, and I don't know if it's your fault or mine, but I just can't do it anymore."

Greg sat still. Claire could see him trying to process all the words she was saying. The moment he realized that the woman sitting across from him was not the woman he'd been eating chicken with for the past couple of decades, she could see it on his face.

"Are you saying you want to divorce?" he asked. His voice was quiet and a little scared.

"No," Claire said. "I'm not saying that. I'm saying I want you to see me. I want you to ask me where I'm going, not when I'm coming back. I want you to notice when I'm wearing a new dress. I want you to know I've been drawing again, and I want you to ask to see what I've drawn. I want you to wonder about me, Greg, on your own, without me telling you to. I want you to be curious about this person you're married to."

The kitchen was so quiet now that Claire could hear the clock on the wall. It was one she'd bought at a craft fair in Beaufort twelve years ago.

Greg looked at his hands. They were resting on either side of his plate. She could see them clearly, his wedding ring, the calluses from yard work, the shape of his fingers that she'd know anywhere, the hands that had held hers thousands of times. He looked older than she usually let herself notice. He had gray at his temples now, lines around his eyes. She did, too. There was a slight heaviness in his shoulders that hadn't been there when they were young.

"I had no idea you were drawing again."

"You didn't ask."

"I didn't know to ask."

"That's the problem, Greg. You don't know because you stopped looking at me a long time ago."

He was quiet. The chicken cooled on their plates. The lighthouse salt shaker stood there, witnessing all of it.

"I don't know how to fix this," he said finally.

"I think we need help," she said. "Professional help. Somebody we can talk to."

"You mean counseling?"

"Yes."

He rubbed the back of his neck. She could see the resistance in his shoulders tightening and his jaw working. Greg definitely didn't believe in counseling. He thought you should deal with everything privately, which meant he believed in not dealing with anything at all. And that's how they had arrived at this table with cold chicken and years of unspoken truth between them.

"I don't know, Claire."

"Greg, I'm just asking you for one thing. One thing in all these years that's just for me. Actually, just for us."

He looked at her. The clock ticked. The refrigerator hummed. The napkin hung on the fridge. Time stood still.

"Okay," Greg said. "Okay, I'll go."

It wasn't a resolution to all the problems. It wasn't even really a breakthrough. It was just a man saying okay, with the enthusiasm of someone who had just agreed to get a root canal. Claire knew that "okay" didn't mean he understood, that he would change, or that the next few months wouldn't be the hardest of their marriage. But right now, okay was what she had.

They sat there. The chicken went cold, and neither of them ate anything. After a while, Greg finally said, "You really started drawing again?"

"Yes."

"Can I see?"

Claire felt a lump in her throat. It was such a small question, but it was the first time in a long time he had asked to see something of hers, something personal.

"Sure," she said. "You can see."

She went to the guest room to retrieve her sketchbook and brought it back to the kitchen table.

She opened it, and Greg started looking at the drawings the way you would look at something you're seeing for the first time, even though it's been right in front of you all along.

There were waves and marshes, the view of the climbing wall, the woman sitting across the table leaning forward, and the Beaufort waterfront at sunset.

He didn't say they were good. He didn't say they were bad. He just turned each page slowly. He closed the book at the end and lifted his head.

"I didn't know," he said. "I should have known, and I didn't. I always loved your drawings, and I never asked over the years why you stopped."

It wasn't an apology, but it was an admission. And Claire could work with that. An admission meant he at least saw the gap, even if he didn't know how to do anything about it.

"We have a lot of work to do," she said.

"Yeah."

"It's gonna be hard."

"Yeah."

"Are you in?"

He looked at the sketchbook and then back at his wife, who was sitting across from him in a green blouse he hadn't complimented, with her Rosewood lipstick he hadn't noticed, and a wave tattoo on her ankle that he had dismissed.

"I'm in."

Claire nodded. She didn't reach for his hand, and he didn't reach for hers. They just sat at the table with the cold chicken and a messy and uncomfortable marriage that was not at all resolved.

But at least it was the most honest they'd been with each other since the night they decided to get married.

She called Harper and Nina at 11 p.m. She sat on her guest room bed with the door closed, the phone on speaker, but her voice low. She told them everything. The cold chicken, the gift card, how she'd been counting to three like a preschooler for years, Greg's face when she showed him her sketchbook. His response that sounded like he was making a dental appointment.

Harper listened without interruption, which was very unusual. Claire almost thought that the call had dropped. When she finished telling them everything, Harper finally spoke.

"He said he'd go to counseling?"

"He said okay, which is not exactly the same thing as an excited agreement."

"Well, I mean, it's Greg. Okay is about as enthusiastic as he gets."

"How do you feel?" Nina asked.

"I feel like I just performed surgery on my own marriage, sitting at the kitchen table with no anesthesia."

"Well, that sounds about right," Harper said.

"But I also feel very relieved," Claire said.

Saying this even surprised her because relief wasn't the emotion she'd expected. She had expected fear, maybe grief or nausea, from saying things she couldn't take back at this point. But beneath it all, she felt a looseness in her chest that hadn't been there before.

"You did a very brave thing," Nina said. "And that's what this whole pact was for, not just so we could go sing karaoke or jump in the ocean. This kind of stuff. This real scary stuff."

"Well, the real scary stuff is a lot scarier than the fun scary stuff we've been doing."

"Always is," Harper said.

They stayed on the phone for about another twenty minutes. Harper told them Jordan had asked her to dinner, a real dinner, not a coffee. She had actually said yes and was trying not to spiral about it. Her voice had a different quality when she talked about Jordan now. It was softer and less guarded.

Nina told them she'd gotten a text from Sam. It wasn't anything dramatic, just, *"I enjoyed meeting you. Would you want to get coffee sometime?"* She hadn't responded to it yet, but she was thinking about it.

"What's to think about?" Harper asked.

"Well, everything. Nothing, actually. I don't know if I'm ready. I don't know if I'm ready or if I feel like I'm ready or if that's something you decide."

"It is something you decide," Claire said. She was now lying on the guest room bed, staring at the ceiling. "Ready isn't something that arrives on a schedule, Nina. It's a thing you choose when you're still scared. Say yes to the coffee, to all of it. Just say yes, and then you can figure out the rest later."

Nina was quiet for a moment. "Okay."

"Wow, we have lots of okays tonight," Harper said. "Greg's okay, Nina's okay. I said yes to dinner. We're making some progress here, people."

"Well, it sure doesn't feel like progress over here," Claire said. "But I do feel like I'm standing on the edge of something, possibly a cliff."

"That's what progress feels like," Nina said. "Trust me, I've been standing on the edge for months. The view is terrifying, but beautiful at times."

They said goodnight. Claire hung up and lay

there for a while longer, listening to the creaks and croaks of her old house. Greg's television was off. The den was dark. In fact, the whole house was dark and quiet.

Somewhere down the hall, her husband was lying in their bed alone, hopefully and probably staring at the ceiling the same way she was. They were in the same house, in the same marriage. And finally, after twenty-six years of chicken and counting to three, they had told each other the truth.

Claire picked up the phone and typed a text to Greg. She deleted it three times before finally settling on,

> Thank you for listening tonight.

His response came after a long pause.

> I'm sorry about the gift card.

She looked at that text for a very long time.

> It's not just about the gift card, Greg.

Another long pause.

It was a small, uncertain beginning, a text at
midnight from the man in the next room who was
trying, clumsily and belatedly, to learn how to see
her, this woman he'd married so long ago.

It wasn't enough, but it was a start.

She put her phone on the nightstand and closed
her eyes. She didn't go to the master bedroom, not
tonight, but she did leave the guest room door open,
which she had never done before.

Nina almost didn't go. She almost didn't go three separate times.

The first time was a week before, when she read the retreat brochure that Claire had found online. The air left her lungs. It was like it was sucked out by one of those really strong vacuum cleaners she couldn't afford.

A weekend of guided grief work in a safe, supportive environment, journaling, sharing, and healing. The word healing made her want to close the laptop and drive to Elena's house and eat as much food as she possibly could without ever thinking about this again.

The second moment was in the morning when she was in her disorganized kitchen, her bag packed, with cold coffee on the counter as she looked out the window at the marsh. The tide was low, revealing larger mud flats and herons searching the shallows. The landscape reflected her feelings - exposed and raw. The tide concealed this, turning it into something beautiful. Without it, the marsh was merely mud and bones. Nina had been living without the tide for nearly two years and wasn't sure she wanted to face a room full of strangers and show them her muddy side.

The third time was in the car, forty-five minutes into the drive to the retreat center just outside Aiken, South Carolina. She turned to Claire in the driver's seat and said, "I can't do this."

Claire just kept driving. She didn't even flinch. She didn't argue. She just kept her eyes on the road and her hands on the wheel.

"Okay, you don't have to."

From the back seat, Harper said nothing.

"Wait, so you're not going to talk me into it?"

"Nope," Claire said. "This one has to be your choice."

Nina looked out the window. Pine trees, red clay, the Lowcountry giving way to the Midlands, the landscape flattening.

She thought about the pact. She thought about karaoke and them on stage, singing so badly. She thought about freezing in the Atlantic. She thought about cooking in Señora Morales's kitchen. She thought about the speed dating and Sam's kind face across the table and about the text she hadn't answered three days later, saying yes to coffee.

She thought about all the edges she'd stood on in the last several months and all the times she had stepped off of them and survived.

"Keep driving," she said.

So Claire kept driving.

The retreat center was a former farmhouse that sat on twenty acres of land outside Aiken. It was surrounded by longleaf pines, and there was a stillness that was so quiet you could hear your own heartbeat. It was a beautiful, uncomplicated place.

The farmhouse was white clapboard with a wide front porch and rocking chairs that nobody was sitting in because everybody was sitting inside in a large room that had been set up with folding chairs arranged in a circle. Everyone was looking at each other, knowing they had a shared wound and weren't yet sure how to prove they trusted each other.

There were a total of twelve people, including

Nina, Claire, and Harper. The others were strangers to them. There was a man who looked to be in his sixties, with a beard and very gentle eyes, sitting with his hands folded in his lap. There was a woman about Nina's age who had short hair and a face that looked like it had been crying recently and would probably cry again soon. A younger woman, maybe in her early thirties, held her phone like a shield and wouldn't make eye contact with anyone. A couple who looked to be in their seventies were sitting side by side but not touching.

The facilitator was a woman named Susie. She was petite, with silver hair, and had a calm, steady presence. She wore no jewelry except a thin gold band on her left hand. Nina noticed it immediately because she still wore hers, too, and she knew what it meant to keep wearing the ring even when there was not a matching one anywhere else in the world.

"Welcome," Susie said.

She didn't smile. It wasn't that kind of a welcome. They weren't having a dinner party. It was the kind of welcome that acknowledged you had come here because something terrible had happened to you, and that now you were brave enough to sit in a circle and not pretend otherwise. It was a welcome to grieve openly and not care if it made anyone else uncomfortable.

"The only rule here is that whatever happens in this room stays in this room. Whatever you feel is allowed and right. Whatever you need to say, you can say it here. And if you don't want to say anything, well, that's allowed too."

Nina sat between Claire and Harper. Claire had her hands folded in her lap the way that she would fold them at PTA meetings. Harper sat with her arms crossed, which was her default position in any room where she felt vulnerable.

They were here because of their pact. Claire and Harper certainly hadn't lost their spouses. They had no reason to be at a grief retreat except that they loved Nina. And the pact said you had to show up, so they had. Nina had told them they didn't actually have to come. They had looked at her as if she had suggested they might just want to stop breathing. They had chosen to do this whole thing together, and they weren't going to let her down now.

Grief was something that everyone would experience at some point in their lives. No one was going to get out of this world without it. Grief was just love with no place to go. That had been said many times by many people, and the only people in the world who don't get the privilege to grieve are the ones who didn't experience enough love.

So Harper and Claire had come in solidarity with

their best friend, knowing that at some point in their lives, if they were lucky enough, they would experience grief because it would mean they had also experienced great love.

This morning was introductions. Each person said their name, who they lost, and how long ago it was. It was terrible, but necessary.

The man with the beard was George. He'd lost his wife, Barbara, three years ago to Alzheimer's disease. The woman with the short hair was Diana. She had lost her son, who was twenty-four years old, in a car accident just eight months ago. She said almost nothing else, and nobody asked her to.

The younger woman was Keisha. She had lost her mother six months ago, and she was so angry about it that it filled the room. Nina recognized that anger because she'd felt it too in those early months, before the anger burned out like a shooting star and then left just numbness behind.

The couple in their seventies were Frank and Rose. They had lost their grandson to leukemia. He was only seven years old. Rose spoke, and Frank just stared at the floor like he wanted to be swallowed up by the earth.

Then it was Nina's turn.

"My name is Nina. I lost my husband, David, two years ago. He had a heart attack. He was forty-eight years old."

She said it simply, the way she had learned to say it without the wobble in her voice. The wobble was still there a little bit, somewhere hiding underneath.

Claire spoke. "I'm Claire, and I'm just here for Nina."

"I'm Harper, same."

Susie nodded, and Nina saw several people in the circle look over at Claire and Harper. Maybe they envied them because they weren't in that room due to losing someone. Or maybe they just wondered who would drive hours on a Saturday to sit in a folding chair in a farmhouse because they loved you.

The morning exercises were structured and careful. Susie guided them through breathing exercises that Nina found surprisingly difficult. Not because breathing was hard, but because being still in a quiet room that was full of grief just made everything feel harder.

She guided them through a visualization where they were asked to picture a place where they felt safe. Nina pictured her kitchen on Edisto at six in the morning with David at the window, coffee in his hand.

She didn't cry, not during the breathing or the visualization. She felt tears building behind her eyes, like pressure behind a dam, but she held them back. Nina's grief had always been a private thing for her. She had no plans to change that now. Elena's grief was a bonfire, but Nina's was a locked room.

After lunch, Susie gave each of them a notebook and a pen.

"This afternoon, I'd like you to write a letter to the person you lost. Say whatever it is that you need to say, whatever you haven't said, whatever you've been holding onto, afraid to speak. You don't have to share it with anybody. If you choose to, there will be time this evening."

Nina looked at the blank page. She had not written a letter to David. She hadn't spoken to him out loud either, not in the way people speak to the dead. Because speaking to David meant acknowledging that he couldn't speak back. She talked about him. She said his name. She told stories. But she did not talk to him, because talking to someone who isn't there is the loneliest thing a person can do.

She picked up the pen.

Nina wrote for two hours straight. She sat on the farmhouse's front porch in one of the rocking chairs and just wrote. Claire and Harper were inside. She could hear them through the open window, their voices low, talking to George and Diana. They were doing what they always did, showing up for people, trying to be present and useful. Nina loved them for it, and she needed to be alone for this anyway.

The letter started formally, which was kind of crazy, because she'd never been formal with David in her life.

Dear David, she wrote.

Then she crossed it out and wrote *David*. Then she crossed that out too, because just his name on the page made her feel like her chest was going to cave in. She sat there with the pen in her hand and crossed out words, staring at her.

Then she finally thought, just start, just start anywhere. He's not going to judge you. He never judged you.

She started with the morning he died. She had never written it down. She had told the story to the police, to the hospital, to Elena, to Claire, and Harper, but she'd never put it on paper, because putting it on paper felt different and permanent.

Speaking was just putting words out into the air, and it dissipated, but the paper stayed.

She wrote about that morning, how normal it was, how impossibly and terrifyingly normal. Coffee, toast, and David kissing her on the forehead on his way out the door, which he did every morning. Putting his hand on her shoulder for half a second. Lucia was already at school, and the house was quiet. Nina was standing at the kitchen window, watching her beloved marsh, thinking about nothing, or maybe thinking about groceries, or maybe thinking about whether she needed to call the plumber about the drip in the bathroom sink. It was just a normal Tuesday, the most normal Tuesday.

Then the phone rang, and a voice she didn't know said words that she couldn't process in the moment. And the normal Tuesday became the day the world ended.

She wrote about the hospital, about the waiting room with its terribly uncomfortable chairs and its horrible coffee, about the flickering bright fluorescent lights that made everything look dead. Elena arrived with her rosary and a fury, because Elena fought grief the way she fought everything, like a gladiator, on her feet with God in one hand and rage in the other.

Claire arrived twenty minutes later, still in her

school clothes with chalk on her fingers. Harper arrived from Charleston wearing heels, having driven ninety miles an hour. Nina knew it because Harper later told her with no apology.

She wrote about the funeral, about Lucia, 14, standing in front of the church in a black dress that was way too big, because who buys a funeral dress for their 14-year-old? She sang the song that David loved, her voice small and clear and absolutely unbearable, and Elena collapsed into the chair afterward and said in Spanish, "My boy, my boy, my beautiful boy."

And Nina holding her because there was nobody else to hold Elena. And holding someone while your own heart is shattering to pieces is the hardest thing Nina has ever done.

She wrote about the after, the cards and casseroles, the people who had said, he's in a better place, trying to mean well, and the people who said, call me if you need anything, and the people who said nothing because they just didn't know what to say, and how people who said nothing were often the ones who helped the most, because at least they didn't ask her to feel grateful that the love of her life, her soulmate, was in a better place that she couldn't see or touch.

She wrote about the numbness, about the glass

wall she lived behind, about the months of going through motions, making the coffee, driving Lucia to school, existing in a life that was completely empty from the inside out, about sitting in parking lots, about the television left on, about leaving his boots by the door because she couldn't move them, because it would mean he was never coming back through it.

And then she wrote about the pact, about the napkin, about Hank's and the karaoke and the way her voice cracked on the high note, but she kept singing, about the polar plunge and the way the cold had shocked her body back into feeling something, about Señora Morales's kitchen and the mole and the index cards, and about how Elena had said, good girl, on the phone, about the tattoo, about his initials on her skin forever, about Asheville and the hotel room and the first night she slept through the night without reaching for him, and about how that made her feel good and guilty, about Sam and his kind face and his garden design for the hospice center, and about the way she had checked his name on that card and felt guilty and free at the same time.

And then she wrote,

I'm learning to live without you. I hate that. I hate every single minute of it, but I'm doing it, David, because I have to. You would be furious with me if I didn't. You would have stood in that kitchen and pointed at the marsh and said, look at that, mi amor. Look at that bird. Look at the sky. How can you not want to be fully alive for all of this?

I want to be alive for this. I want to be alive for Lucia and for Elena and for Claire and Harper and for myself. And maybe Sam, who seems kind and patient and doesn't try to replace you, because no one could. He understands that without being told. And maybe not even for him. Maybe it will be someone else down the road. I just don't know.

I love you, and I will always love you. But I can't sit in parking lots anymore. I'm not going to leave the television on. I'm going to cook your grandmother's recipes and teach them to Lucia. I'll put those index cards in a box with your name on it so that a hundred years from now, someone in your family will make mole negro and it will taste like you.

I'm keeping your boots by the door because I'm not ready to move them yet. But I'm going to leave the door open now, David. I'm leaving it open.

She put the pen down. Her hand was cramping, and her face was wet. She didn't even know when the tears had started, but they had, because the page was spotted with them, the ink blurred in places. And she didn't care.

David would have said the best letters are the ones you can't read through your tears.

She read the letter that evening. She hadn't intended to, but Susie said sharing was optional, and Nina had spent the afternoon fully intending to keep that letter very private, folded up in her notebook between herself, David, and the rocking chair.

When George read his letter to Barbara, his voice broke on her name, but he continued. It was so brave and bare that Nina felt something shift inside of her. Diana read her letter to her son. It was only four sentences long, but it destroyed the entire room. And Keisha, who had been angry all day, read a letter to her mother that began, "I'm so mad at you for leaving," and ended, "but I understand why you were tired, and I forgive you." The room was weeping; everyone was even, and Harper, who was crying silently with her arms still crossed, had tears streaming down her face. Susie looked at Nina, and Nina just instinctively stood up.

She stood up and walked to the center of the circle, unfolded the letter, and read it all. The normal Tuesday, what happened at the hospital, Elena and her rosary, Lucia singing at the funeral, the numbness she felt, the parking lots, the television she left on. And then the pact, the karaoke, the mole, the tattoo, the boots still sitting by the door.

Her voice broke several times, but she kept going. She read it the way she'd sung at Hank's, badly but bravely, and all the way through.

When she finished, the room was silent. It wasn't the silence of a polite audience, but a sacred silence of people who had just witnessed something important and true. George was nodding. Diana was holding her notebook against her chest. And Frank, who hadn't spoken all day, looked at Nina and said, "Thank you."

His voice was rough like sandpaper, so full of grief that was old and had become a part of him. Nina understood that "thank you" meant you were saying the thing I couldn't say. She nodded back.

She then sat down, and Claire and Harper were on either side of her. She felt Claire's arm around her shoulders and Harper's hand on her knee, and that is what broke her.

It wasn't the controlled crying she'd done at Señora Morales's stove. It wasn't the quiet tears she normally let fall on the porch. These were full, uncontained, animal-grief tears she'd been holding back behind that wall for two years. Sounds came out of her that she didn't recognize, guttural sounds below language, below thought, just the raw noise of her body finally releasing what it had been carrying for far too long.

She bent forward in the folding chair. Claire and Harper held onto her. The room held onto her. These twelve strangers, two friends, and a facilitator who knew the most important thing that she could do right now was just let it happen.

It lasted a long time, longer than Nina thought possible. And when she was done, she felt like her insides had been emptied out and scrubbed clean.

Susie brought her some water, and George handed her tissues. Diana, who had barely spoken to Nina, came and sat on the floor next to her and held her hand without saying a word.

Nina now understood this was what grief communities were for. They weren't there to fix each other. They weren't even there to make it better. They were just there to sit on the floor and hold hands and say, I know, I know, I've been there, and you're not alone in this.

They drove home in the pitch dark. Claire drove, Harper sat in the passenger seat, and Nina lay in the back with her head against the window, watching the darkened trees slide by. She felt lighter than she had in two years. She wasn't happy. She wasn't healed. She just felt lighter, as if she'd been carrying a really heavy suitcase she didn't know she could set down, and someone had finally said to her, *"You can set that down now. It'll still be there when you need it."*

Nobody said a word for a long time. The road unwound through the dark, past small towns with gas stations and church steeples, past fields that were invisible at night, but Nina could feel.

"Thank you," Nina said. Her voice was hoarse at this point. She sounded like she'd been crying for an hour, which, of course, she had. "For coming and being there for me. For all of it."

"You don't need to thank us," Harper said.

Harper had cried in that room and had not fully recovered from the indignity, which Nina found both touching and hilarious.

"Harper cried," Claire said, because Claire was not going to let that go without being noticed.

"I had an allergic reaction."

"To what?"

"Emotions. I'm allergic to emotions. It's a confirmed medical condition."

Nina laughed. It was the best laugh she'd had in months, even better than the one at Hank's, because this one came from a place that had been emptied out. It could hold this, too. She'd proven that the emptiness could hold more than grief. It could also hold laughter and love and the particular joy of being in a car at ten o'clock at night with two women who had sat on a floor and held her while she fell apart, but were now making jokes about it because that was what thirty years of friendship had earned you. The right to laugh at each other during the worst moments. And no, the laughter wasn't a betrayal.

Claire dropped Harper at her building in Charleston. Through the car window, Nina could see Harper's light in the condo. She could hear music playing faintly through the open balcony door.

"Jordan's up there," Claire said as they pulled away.

"How do you know?"

"The music. Harper doesn't play music when she's alone or not at home."

They drove to Edisto. The bridge was dark, the marsh invisible, headlights carving the road out of nothing. Nina's house appeared at the end of the drive with the porch light on, which meant Elena had left it on because Elena always left the porch light on when Nina was gone, the same way she'd left it on for David.

Nina got out of the car. She stood in the driveway, breathing in the marsh air. This was the smell of her life, the life she had shared with David, and now the new life she was learning to live without him.

She went inside. The house was quiet, but it felt less empty, as if a room had been cleared out to make space for something new. She walked past David's boots by the back door. She didn't move them. She wasn't ready. But she looked at them and thought, *I told you I'd leave the door open. I meant it.*

And then she picked up her phone and texted Sam.

> I'd like to have dinner sometime, not just coffee. Dinner, if you're interested.

His response came within three minutes.

> I'm very interested. You pick the place.

Nina put her phone on the counter. She looked at

the marsh out the kitchen window, the place that David had fallen in love with years ago. She couldn't see it at night, but she could feel it.

She made a cup of coffee, even though it was ten-thirty at night, and she would never go to sleep. She sat at the kitchen table and drank it slowly, looking out the dark window, and she didn't turn on the television.

The house was very quiet, but for the first time, quiet didn't hurt.

CHAPTER 13

Harper had only five minutes of material prepared and was utterly terrified through-out. She wasn't someone who became scared easily and couldn't even recall the last time she felt the word 'terrified'.

She was the person who gave presentations every quarter to a board of directors that controlled billions of dollars and whose idea of a warm greeting was a firm handshake.

She had pitched acquisitions in rooms where a single wrong number would mean someone's career ended. She had negotiated contracts across time zones and languages she didn't even speak, with the help of translators who looked more nervous than she did.

Harper Ellis didn't get terrified. She just got prepared.

But here she was, sitting on her couch in Charleston at nine o'clock on a Thursday night, reading her notes for the fifth time, and her hands were shaking. Not because the material was bad, just because the material was actually true.

This was her pick for the ninth month: an open mic comedy night at a small club in Charleston called The Laff Stop. It was spelled exactly that way, which Harper found offensive on a grammatical level, but she had chosen it because it hosted an open mic night every Friday that, according to the reviews, was welcoming and not too intimidating.

She picked stand-up because, after the grief retreat, she had told Claire and Nina that they needed a good laugh. Claire had said, "Then let's just go see a comedy." And Harper said, "That's not scary. Let's go *do* comedy."

The words had left her mouth before her brain had time to file a formal objection.

The thing about stand-up was that it required you to be honest about your life in front of a group of strangers and then make them laugh about it, laugh at you.

Harper was very good at making people laugh. She was sharp and quick-witted. Her timing was impeccable. And she had been the funniest person in every room she'd entered since she was about fourteen years old.

But being funny in a boardroom was very different than being funny up on stage. Being funny on stage was like standing in front of a bunch of people without your clothes on. And although Harper kept in shape and was proud of her body, she did not want to stand in front of a group of people without her clothes on.

In her boardrooms, humor was armor. On a stage, humor was the wound.

Her material was about being single, childless, a woman in finance, about eating toast over the sink, about her mother calling to report cousin Margaux's reproductive achievements, about the fiddle leaf fig that her assistant kept alive because she just couldn't be trusted with a houseplant. It was also about what it meant that the longest relationship in her life was with a man named James, who watered her plants on Wednesdays.

It was funny. She knew it was funny because she'd read it to James, and he'd laughed so hard he'd spilled his coffee on the desk. Then he said, "Please don't fire me for laughing at the part about your love life."

Harper had said, "You laugh every day at my love life, James. That's not new."

But the funny wasn't the hard part. The hard part was the truth beneath the funny. The loneliness she turned into a punchline.

Her phone buzzed. It was Jordan.

> Good luck tonight. You're going to be great.

She had told him about the pact. She'd told him about all of it over three different dinners and four coffees and a walk along the Battery that lasted over two hours and ended with him holding her hand. She had let him, which was the most significant physical contact Harper had had with another human since the polar plunge. And the polar plunge had been with the Atlantic Ocean.

> If I say I did terribly, you are obligated to lie and say I was great.

> I've never lied to you, and I'm not starting tonight, but you won't be terrible.

Harper stared at the text and thought about the word never.

Jordan had never lied to her. He had never told her she was easy to love because she wasn't. And they both knew it.

But what he had said four years ago, the night that she ended it, standing in his workshop in Mount Pleasant with sawdust on the floor and a half-finished rocking chair between them, was, "You're worth the difficulty, Harper. I just wish you would believe that."

She was trying to believe that. She was trying so hard to believe that.

The Laff Stop was located in a basement on King Street, where the smell of popcorn and sweat hung in the air. It was small. There were maybe eighty seats, and most of them were folding chairs that had seen better days. They were arranged in front of a stage that was the size of a closet, with a single microphone and a spotlight.

The walls were exposed brick, covered in framed headshots of comedians who had apparently performed here on the way to somewhere else. This definitely wasn't a destination club.

The bar in the back served beer and wine, and

something called a Laff Attack that looked like a margarita mixed with several other drinks.

Claire was already there, sitting at a table in the front with a notebook. Because, of course, Claire would bring a notebook. Claire had written her material on index cards, organized them by topic, and practiced them in front of her bathroom mirror.

Harper loved her level of preparation. She brought it to every activity that was supposed to feel like something you didn't prepare for.

Nina arrived looking better than she had in months, better than she had even since the pact started. There was a quality to her that was hard to name. Not happiness, but more like presence. Like she was back. Like she had gone somewhere that grief had taken her, and she was now back home, fully.

She was wearing color, a deep blue top that wasn't David's.

"There are eight people signed up before us," Claire said, looking at her notebook. "We are numbers nine, ten, and eleven. Average set is five minutes, so that gives us about forty minutes to prepare."

"Forty minutes to sit here in absolute horrifying terror," Harper said.

"Well, that too."

"So what's your material about?" Nina asked Claire.

Claire looked at her index cards. "Parenting, marriage, being a third-grade teacher who organizes her pantry for fun."

"You're using the pantry?"

"Well, the pantry's funny. I organized it alphabetically, then by food group, and my husband never noticed either time. I think that's pretty good material."

"What about you?" Harper asked Nina.

Nina was quiet for a moment. "I'm going to talk about David."

They all went still.

"I'm going to tell the story about the pelicans," Nina said. "How he used to watch them fish and say they were proof you didn't have to be graceful to be effective. And then the story about the time he tried to cook Thanksgiving dinner by himself and set off every single smoke detector in the house. And then the fire department came, and he offered them turkey."

"He did not," Harper said.

"He absolutely did. And the fire chief even stayed for pie."

Harper bit the inside of her cheek to keep from laughing. Nina was sitting in a comedy club talking about her dead husband, and she was glowing. Things sure had changed in the last few months.

The eight comics before them ranged from painfully terrible to surprisingly good. There was a college kid who did five minutes about his roommate's sleep talking that was funnier than it had any right to be. Then there was a woman in her thirties who talked about online dating with deadpan delivery. It kind of reminded Harper of herself.

A man in a Hawaiian shirt told dad jokes. The audience laughed, not at the jokes, but at his sheer force of belief in them. A woman bombed so terribly that the room went quiet and then, in an act of collective mercy, gave her a standing ovation, which made her cry, then made everyone else cry.

Then the host called Claire's name.

Claire stood up. She smoothed out her blouse, picked up her index cards, and walked up to the stage like she was about to conduct a school assembly. That was the only public-speaking context she had, and Harper watched with a mixture of love and dread.

Claire tapped the microphone.

"Hi, I'm Claire. I'm a third-grade teacher, a wife, and a mother. I'm fifty years old. And the most rebellious thing I've ever done in the last twenty-six years is organize my pantry."

There were a few polite laughs.

Claire looked down at her index cards. Then she put them on the stool and kept talking without them, which was so unlike Claire that Harper actually sat up straight in her chair.

"So my husband gave me a gift card for my fiftieth birthday, not to a store, one of those universal gift cards, you know, the kind that says, oh, I can't be bothered to have a single thought about what you might enjoy. It was thirty dollars, but I can go to any participating retailer. Happy half a century of being alive, honey. Go buy yourself something at Walgreens."

The room laughed. It was a real laugh.

Claire's eyes went wide for a second.

"I've been sleeping in the guest room for two months. And you know what my husband said? Nothing. He said absolutely nothing. In two months, this man has not even asked me a single question about why I moved out of our bedroom. I could be building a spaceship in there. I could be running an underground poker ring, and he would definitely not notice."

More laughter, louder this time.

Claire was finding her rhythm.

She talked about the napkin color crisis. She talked about counting to three before responding to her husband and how she had counted to three approximately 47,550 times in her marriage, which, at three seconds each, was roughly 39 hours of her life spent not saying what she actually thought.

"You know, that's almost two full days. I've spent two days of my life biting my tongue. I have a groove right here," she said, opening her mouth and sticking out her tongue.

The room was with her now. Harper could feel it. The laughter stopped being polite and started being real.

Claire finally ended her set.

"But I'm learning. I'm fifty, and I'm learning to say the first thing instead of the third thing. It's kind of scary. My husband is just confused. My friends are delighted, and my pantry is still very much organized by food group because some things are just correct."

The applause was warm and genuine and seemed to last longer than Claire was prepared for. She picked up her index cards, which she hadn't used at all, and walked back to the table with a dazed expression on her face.

Harper squeezed her arm. "You didn't use the cards."

"I know. I don't know what happened. I just opened my mouth, and the truth fell out."

"That's called comedy, Claire."

Nina went next. She walked up onto the stage timidly, the way she did everything, with intention rather than hesitation. A woman who was moving toward something now instead of away from it. She adjusted the microphone to her shorter stature and looked out at the room.

"My husband David died two years ago."

The room went very quiet, very quickly.

"He was forty-eight years old. Heart attack. Completely sudden. One morning, he was making us coffee. The next morning, I was making coffee alone. And the coffee tasted exactly the same, which means my husband wasn't as great as I thought he was at making coffee."

There was a short beat and then a small laugh, an uncertain one. The audience wasn't even sure they were allowed to laugh at this. Nina smiled, which gave them permission.

"David was Mexican, and his mother Elena is,

and I mean this with all the love in my heart, the most intense woman in the southeastern United States. When her son died, Elena showed up at my house with enough food to feed the entire island I live on, and the opinion that I was definitely not grieving correctly. According to Elena, there is a correct way to grieve. It involves eating a lot, crying very loudly, and going to church, sometimes doing all three things simultaneously. I was doing zero of these things, which made her completely horrified."

The room was laughing now. Nina was talking with a steadiness and a warmth.

"David used to watch the pelicans on our dock, and he would sit there for hours and watch them dive for fish. Have you ever watched a pelican fish? It's like watching someone very uncoordinated belly flop into a pool, but still come up with dinner. Absolutely no grace whatsoever. Just commitment and a very big mouth. If you've been to a buffet, you know what I mean."

She paused.

"David said pelicans were proof that you didn't have to be graceful to be effective. I think he might have been talking about himself because he was a man who once tried to cook the entire Thanksgiving dinner by himself and then set off every smoke alarm in the house. The fire department came. David offered them turkey, and the fire chief stayed for pie."

The room erupted in laughter. It was more of a joyful laugh, like hearing a story about someone you'd never met and loving them instantly.

"I miss him every day," Nina said. "But I'm learning to live without him, and it turns out that living without someone you love is a lot like watching a pelican fish. There's no grace, but full commitment, and a big mouth when necessary."

She walked off the stage with the loudest applause of the night.

Claire was crying. Harper wasn't crying because Harper had used up her annual tear allocation at the grief retreat and was now operating on her emotional reserves.

Nina sat down.

"David was unbelievable," Harper said, smiling.

"David was the best person I've ever known," Nina said.

Now she was smiling. Not that ghost of a smile, not a forced one, but a real one. The one who had been gone for two years and was back now.

Harper went last. She walked onto the stage and adjusted the microphone. She looked at the audience. She was wearing silk, as she pretty much always did, and her heels were too tall for the basement club. Her hair was perfect, and she looked like a woman who had wandered into the wrong building.

"Good evening," she said. "My name is Harper. I'm the vice president of a financial division that manages $200 million. I have a corner office on the 14th floor. I drive a perfect German car. I own exactly one houseplant, which my assistant waters because I can't be trusted with living things."

She paused for a moment.

"I eat toast over the kitchen sink for dinner because I don't even own a table. It's not because I can't afford a table. I mean, I just told you what my job is, but because buying a table would mean admitting that I'm always eating alone, and I would just rather eat standing up than sit down with that information."

The room was quiet, like they were holding their breath.

"My mom calls me three times a week to tell me about other people's children. She never says I should have children. She just mentions that her friend Bitsy's daughter just had twins, or that cousin

Margaux is on her second, or that the surgeon at church is tall and recently divorced. She delivers the information the way a meteorologist delivers a storm warning, repeatedly, factually, and with the implication that I should be doing something about it."

Laughter. Half the room must have had a mother like Harper's.

"The closest thing I have to a long-term relationship is with my assistant, James. James waters my plant. He knows my coffee order. He once told my mother I was in a meeting when I was actually just eating a burrito in my car because I couldn't face another phone call about cousin Margaux and her highly effective ovaries. James has an emotional support ferret named Dolores who sits in a carrier under his desk and judges everyone who walks past. So Dolores and I have a lot in common, actually. We're both very judgmental, and we both pretend that we don't need anyone while secretly hoping someone will pick us. Oh, and we both bite when necessary."

The room was hers. Harper felt it the way she did in a board meeting when everything tipped in her direction and the numbers and universe suddenly aligned. Except this wasn't about numbers. This was about standing in the spotlight and telling the truth about her life and turning the loneliest parts of it into something that made strangers laugh.

She told them about the pact, about the three of them turning fifty and deciding to stop being careful, about karaoke at a bar with peanut shells on the floor, about running into the ocean in their matching polka-dot bathing suits, about getting a tattoo on her wrist, a tiny little wave.

"And here's the part that scares me most," she said. "There's a man, a really good man. He builds furniture with his hands, knows how I take my coffee, and once told me I was worth the trouble I caused. But I pushed him away years ago because I was scared. And now he's back, and he's patient, and he's waiting, and here I am standing on a stage in a basement in Charleston telling all these strangers about him before I've actually told him."

She paused. The room was completely still.

"So if anyone sees a man in Mount Pleasant with sawdust on his jeans and a rocking chair in his workshop, you tell him that Harper said she's ready to buy a kitchen table."

The room went crazy with applause, a full, unrestrained roar from an audience who had just heard something brave.

Harper stood there in the spotlight and felt it

wash over her. She walked back to the table. Claire was grinning, and Nina was wiping her eyes.

"A kitchen table?" Claire asked.

"It's just a metaphor."

"It's not a metaphor, Harper. It's actual furniture. Are you going to buy a kitchen table?"

"Actually, I think I'm gonna let him build me one."

Claire and Nina looked at each other, and that said everything. Harper saw it and rolled her eyes before taking a sip of wine. Her heart was still pounding.

She picked up the phone under the table and typed.

> Jordan, I know it's late. I just did something brave and stupid. Can I come over?

His response took twelve seconds.

> The door has been open for four years, Harper. Come home.

She didn't show anyone the text. She just put the phone in her pocket and sat there with her two best friends, ordering another round and laughing about the man in the Hawaiian shirt, Claire's index cards, and the fire chief who stayed for pie.

When they left at midnight, Harper drove straight to Mount Pleasant instead of back to her condo. She parked in Jordan's driveway. The workshop light was on. She could hear music through the open door, something low and acoustic, and see his shadow moving inside.

She sat in her car for about thirty seconds, the time it took to run into the Atlantic, and then got out and walked toward the light.

CHAPTER 14

Nina had a date on Saturday. Not this Saturday. This Saturday was the pact for month ten: horseback riding on a trail outside Beaufort. It was Claire's pick. But her date was next Saturday, and it was a real date at a restaurant on Shem Creek that Sam had chosen because it had a patio overlooking the water.

Nina had told him during one of their long phone calls over the past few weeks that she liked eating near water. He had remembered.

That was the thing about Sam. He remembered things.

They'd had coffee three times, dinner once at a quiet place on James Island where Sam lived. He had a small house with a garden he had designed himself. Nina had seen photographs on his phone.

Sam was organized and intentional. Nina's garden on Edisto was a patch of dirt that David used to tend, but had gone feral in the two years since he had died. She was no gardener.

Sam was patient in a way Nina found deeply disarming. He didn't push. He didn't fill silences with chatter. He just sat across from her, listening with the attention of a man who designed landscapes for a living and understood that the best things needed time and space to grow.

He'd lost his wife, Beth, to cancer a couple of years ago, and his grief was different from Nina's. It was quieter, more settled, like a river that flowed steadily rather than flooding.

He never tried to compare their losses. He didn't try to bond over their shared pain. He just sat there, warm and present, and let her be wherever she was at that moment.

The guilt was fading a bit. It wasn't gone. Nina thought that the guilt would probably never be completely gone, the way a scar doesn't always fully disappear, but it had softened into something that she could carry without it crushing her soul.

She had talked about it with Susie at the retreat and then with Elena, who had surprised her by saying, "David loved you enough to want you to be happy, even without him. Don't you dare insult him by refusing to be."

Elena had said it fiercely, but that was the way she said everything. And then she had changed the subject to the quality of the tomatoes at the Piggly Wiggly. They were apparently mushy that week, and this was unacceptable.

Lucia did have opinions about Sam. Of course, Lucia also had opinions about everything. But her opinions about Sam seemed cautiously positive. She'd only met him once, and very briefly, when he came to pick up Nina for coffee.

They stood on the porch on Edisto, making small talk, while Lucia looked at him from the doorway.

Afterward, Lucia had said, "He seems okay."

"Just okay?" Nina asked.

"He's not Dad."

"No one is Dad," Nina said.

"I know, but he seems like a person who might be nice to you, and that's really what matters."

Lucia had paused.

"Also, his shoes were clean. Dad always said you can tell a lot about a person just from looking at their shoes."

"Your dad wore flip-flops nine months of the year."

"Dad was an exception to his own rules. That was part of his charm," Lucia said, giggling.

The trail ride was at a stable outside Beaufort. The property backed up to the Coosaw River and stretched through a forest so thick with live oaks and Spanish moss that the light came through in shafts. It was green and gold and quiet, like a cathedral.

Claire had found the place online, of course. She'd read fourteen reviews, called the owner twice, and confirmed that the horses were gentle and the trails were scenic. She also wanted to make sure there was no prior experience required, since none of them had any.

Nina had been on a horse one time at a birthday party when she was nine. The horse had walked in a circle in a fenced ring for ten minutes, and she thought it was the most thrilling experience of her life.

Harper had never been on a horse and had said, when told about this month's adventure, "I manage $200 million portfolios. I can certainly manage a horse."

Claire had decided not to respond to this comment.

The stable owner was a woman named Gail, with a weathered face and the authority of someone who had definitely spent her life taking care of more animals than people. She wore boots and a sun-bleached hat and spoke to the horses in a low voice that suggested they were her preferred conversation partners.

"This one's Clementine," Gail said, bringing a brown mare to Nina. "She's steady. She won't spook, and she's a good listener." She looked at Nina. "You ride before?"

"Once, when I was nine. Um, it was a pony."

"Close enough," Gail said, handing her the reins. "Just let her know you're there. She'll do the rest."

Claire got a dappled gray one named Biscuit, which she found very delightful.

Harper got a tall bay named General, which she found terrifying. "We will understand each other," Harper told the horse. It was more of a demand than anything else.

General blinked at her, probably not impressed by her corporate title.

They mounted with varying degrees of grace. Nina managed it on the second try. Claire needed a stepstool and encouragement from Gail, who said to just swing her leg over like she was getting onto a tall bicycle. That was only helpful if you had spent your whole life riding tall bicycles.

Harper mounted General with the confidence of a woman who had maybe watched a YouTube video the night before and thought she was fully trained.

"Y'all ready?" Gail asked from her own horse, which was a calm black gelding.

"Ready," Nina said.

They entered the trail.

The forest closed around them. Live oaks arched overhead, their branches heavy with moss. The path was wide enough for two horses side by side. The ground was just packed dirt and sand, and the only sounds were the clop of hooves and the occasional crack of a branch somewhere in the canopy above, which was a little scary.

The river appeared through breaks in the trees, smelling of salt and mud and that particular Lowcountry sweet smell of late summer.

Nina found that being on a horse was its own kind of meditation. The rhythm of Clementine's walk was steady and hypnotic, and it loosened places in Nina's body she didn't even know were tight. She wasn't in control. The horse was in control. All Nina had to do was sit and move with it and trust that Clementine knew exactly where she was going.

There was a lesson in that, probably. Nina was learning not to force lessons anymore. They came when they came.

They rode in single file through a narrow stretch. Moss hung so low that it brushed their shoulders. Nobody talked for a full five minutes, but it wasn't an empty silence. It was the kind of silence that only exists in nature. Nina breathed it in and felt her chest expand.

The trail widened at a clearing near the riverbank, and Gail stopped and told them they could walk the horses side by side for a while. Nina brought Clementine alongside Claire's Biscuit, and Harper guided General up the other side. And the three of them rode together through the forest with the river on their left and the moss above, the August sun warm on their shoulders.

"This is the most peaceful thing we've done," Claire said. Her voice was low.

"It's the least terrifying thing we've done," Harper said.

"Is that a complaint?"

"No, I'm just saying that I'm on a horse in a forest

and I'm not screaming for my life. So this is progress."

General snorted, which made it seem like he was laughing at them.

They rode in silence for another stretch as the river widened and osprey circled overhead, folding their wings, diving, and coming up with fish. Nina thought about the pelicans and David. The way that the Lowcountry seemed to always teach her the same lesson. Commit, dive, trust that there's something down there worth reaching for.

"So Greg and I started counseling," Claire said.

Nina and Harper both looked at her. Claire was staring at the path ahead, one hand on the reins and the other resting on her thigh. She sat differently now, taller, less folded up, like a woman who remembered she was allowed to take up space in the world.

"How is it?" Nina asked.

"Hard, really hard. He cries. I guess I didn't expect that. He sits in the therapist's office and cries. Turns out Greg has been carrying things too. Things I didn't know about because I was so busy being invisible. I forgot that he might be feeling invisible too."

Somewhere, a woodpecker was methodically

trying to dismantle a tree. The horses continued walking, and the moss continued swaying.

"He told the therapist about the gift card," Claire said, "about how he didn't even choose a store. And then he said, 'I didn't know what she wanted. I haven't known what she wanted in years. And I was afraid to ask because I was afraid the answer would be something I couldn't give her.'"

Nina let that settle in for a moment. It was more complicated than she had expected the answer to be. She had been ready to dislike Greg for most of this year. She'd been quietly building her case against him in her head. But this was a different picture. Not a man who didn't care, but maybe a man who was scared.

"Is it helping?" Harper asked.

"I don't know yet. It's only been three sessions, but he did ask to see my sketchbook again last week, unprompted. He sat on the couch, and he looked at every page. He asked me about the marsh painting, a new one I was doing, one I did in watercolor. He even asked what time of day it was."

"What time was it?" Nina asked.

"Sunrise. I painted it from memory, from the mornings when I sat on the porch before school. I loved to watch the light rise up from over the river."

She paused for a moment. "He said, 'I didn't know you got up that early.' And I said, 'I've been getting up that early for fifteen years, Greg.' He looked at me, and I could see it, the moment that he understood there was this entire version of me that he hadn't been noticing."

The trail curved through a stand of palmetto palms, and a blue heron lifted off from the shallow water near the bank.

"Are you staying?" Nina asked.

Of course, she meant in the marriage. She meant in the house, in the life, in this thing that they'd built so many years ago. She'd been afraid to ask the question because she also knew Claire was probably afraid to answer.

"I'm trying," Claire said. "I mean, we're both trying. It's awkward and messy. I moved back into the bedroom last week, and it felt like sleeping next to a stranger."

"That's an upsetting thing to say about someone you've been married to for twenty-six years, but it's honest," Harper said.

"Yeah, well, honesty is exhausting sometimes. I understand why I counted to three for so long. It's so much easier to just say the safe thing."

"Easier isn't always better," Nina said.

"No, it's not."

"Easy is what keeps you stuck," Harper said under her breath.

Claire looked over at the river. Nina recognized something on her face because she herself had worn it for over two years. It was the expression of a woman standing in the middle of her life, looking at a mess and wondering if she was capable of cleaning it up or if it was just easier to walk away.

They stopped at a bluff overlooking the river to take a break. Gail tied the horses to a low branch and handed out water bottles she'd brought in her saddlebag. The three of them sat like kids, with their feet dangling over the bluff and looking at the Coosaw River spread out below.

"Harper update," Nina said.

This had become a tradition because Harper would not volunteer personal information unprompted. You had to ask her. You had to request the Harper report, and even then, she would usually heavily edit it before delivery.

Harper took a drink of water and looked at the river. She was quiet for long enough that Nina started to wonder if she was going to decline the comment at all, which was Harper's constitutional right and one that she liked to exercise frequently.

"I'm spending Sundays at Jordan's," she finally said.

Claire's water bottle froze halfway to her mouth.

"Sundays?" Claire said, "Like as in every Sunday?"

"As in six Sundays in a row, as in it's on my calendar with no end date, as in I have a coffee mug there and a drawer. He gave me a drawer."

Harper said this as though she were receiving some special award, which, for Harper, she supposed, she was.

"He cleared out the bottom left drawer in his kitchen and put a box of chamomile tea in it because I mentioned one time, in passing, in a sentence I don't even really remember finishing, that I drink chamomile in the evening. He turned a sentence into a drawer. He said, 'This is yours.' And just like that, like it was nothing. Like giving someone space in your kitchen is not the most intimate thing a person can do."

"It's a drawer, Harper," Nina said gently.

"It's not just a drawer. It's a declaration. A drawer says, 'I expect you to come back.' A drawer says, 'There is room for you here.' A drawer says, 'I am planning for your presence in my life.'" She paused. "I've never had a drawer."

Nina looked at Harper, sitting on the bluff in riding boots she'd bought specifically for today. She had exchanged her silk blouse for a cotton shirt because even Harper couldn't justify riding on horseback with a silk blouse on. She thought about that woman who, months ago, was eating toast over the kitchen sink, who had deleted Jordan's messages, who had kept everyone at arm's length and thought it was strength. That woman would have never accepted a drawer.

"Does he make you happy?" Nina asked.

Harper looked at the river again. A shrimp boat passed slowly, its nets folded.

"He cooks for me," Harper said. "Every Sunday, he starts in the morning, and by the time I get there, the whole house smells like rosemary and garlic. And then he puts it all on the table, not on a counter, a table. He has a kitchen table, Nina, with chairs, four of them."

Her voice had gone quiet.

"And he's building me a table," Harper said, "for my place, out of reclaimed wood from an old church in Georgetown that was torn down last year. He's been working on it in the evenings. He sends me a picture every night, just the wood, where he is in the process."

She took a breath.

"It's the most romantic thing anyone has ever done for me, and it's a piece of furniture."

"It's not just a piece of furniture," Claire said.

Gail appeared behind them, leading the horses.

"Y'all ready to head back? We got about a mile."

They mounted up. The trail wound through the thickest part of the forest, where the oaks were the oldest and the moss hung the heaviest. It was like riding through a tunnel of green.

Nina rode behind Claire and in front of Harper. She watched Claire's back, straight and steady on Biscuit, and listened to General's breathing behind her. She thought about the pact, the napkin, the mole, the karaoke, the freezing ocean, Elena's casseroles, and Lucia's honesty. She thought about Sam's patience, and then she thought about the two with her, Claire and Harper, who had shown up at every edge and stood beside her and jumped.

The stable appeared through the trees. They dismounted and returned the horses. Clementine nudged Nina's shoulder with her nose before being led away. Gail said that meant she liked her, and Nina chose to believe that a horse's opinion was just as good as anyone else's.

They stood in the stable yard for a while, looking at the river glinting through the trees. The air smelled like horse and hay.

"Two more," Claire said, "just two more adventures."

"Painting class next month," Nina said, "then the big one."

"Skydiving," Harper said, her nose scrunching upward.

"We don't need to talk about the skydiving yet," Claire said.

"Oh, we absolutely have to talk about skydiving. We need to talk about it extensively because we have to prepare."

"Harper, we rode horses today. We're still standing in the stable. Can we just have five minutes before we start planning to jump to our deaths out of an airplane?"

"Five minutes," Harper agreed. "Then we plan."

Nina smiled. She looked at her friends. She had been a woman who almost hadn't even come to Claire's birthday party ten months ago. She had been a woman who sat in parking lots. She had been a woman who couldn't feel anything. That woman would never have ridden a horse through a forest or had a date planned for Saturday. She wouldn't have a letter to David folded in her nightstand or a jar of Señora Morales' salsa in her fridge. She wouldn't have a wave with initials on her wrist.

She was still that woman, but she was also

someone new. She could be both things at once, it seemed.

"Let's go get lunch," Nina said. "I'm starving."

They walked to Claire's car, three women in riding boots, smelling like horses, squinting in the sun. This road they came in on would also lead them to their next adventure and the one after that, and whatever came after the pact, which they were all beginning to understand was just more life, more living, more of the things they had almost forgotten how to do simply because their ages had changed.

The therapist's name was Dr. Lydia Warren, and she had that particular gift of saying very little but making you say everything. Her office was in a small building in Beaufort, on the second floor, with a window that looked out over the live oaks lining the sidewalk. The room was painted a soft, calming blue, calming or depressing, depending on Claire's mood. There was a couch with two chairs and a box of tissues on the end table, a clock on the wall that ticked quietly, counting down the fifty minutes Claire and Greg spent here every Thursday at four o'clock.

They sat at opposite ends of the couch, like strangers on a bus. They were on session six, and it was not going well. It was not going badly; it was just going the way the therapist had warned it would go, slowly, painfully, with lots of silence.

Greg handled the silence better than Claire expected. He sat on his end of the couch, hands on his knees, and answered all the doctor's questions with careful deliberation. This was the first time in his adult life he had been asked to examine the inner workings of his mind, and he seemed to find the process unfamiliar, but he didn't deflect. He didn't make jokes. He just sat there and tried.

On Greg, trying looked like a man learning a language he should have learned twenty years earlier, slowly sounding out all the words and getting some of them wrong, but he still showed up every week.

Claire had learned that their marriage hadn't gotten into this mess without her making some mistakes along the way, too. And it was hard to change ingrained patterns, but she was trying.

Today, Dr. Warren asked each of them to describe what they wanted the marriage to look like a year from now.

Greg had gone first. He'd stared at the carpet for a long time, and Claire had watched the side of his face, trying to process in his brain something he'd never been asked to do before.

"I want to eat dinner together," he'd finally said,

"at the table, not with me in the den and her in the kitchen, but together. And I want to know what she's thinking about while we eat."

Dr. Warren looked at Claire. "And you?"

Claire had looked at Greg, at his hands on his knees, at the gray around his temples and the lines around his eyes. He was wearing a College of Charleston T-shirt, the same one he'd worn to her birthday dinner almost a year ago, which she now realized was just probably his favorite shirt, and she'd never even asked him about it.

"I want to be surprised," she had said. "I want him to surprise me, not with a gift, just with a question I don't expect or a thought he hasn't shared. I want to sit across from my husband and discover something about him that I didn't know."

Dr. Warren let the silence sit. The clock ticked in the background.

"You know what's funny?" Greg said, still looking at the carpet. "I've been watching the Braves since 1995. Almost thirty years, same team, same replay, same highlight reels. I just realized I've been doing the same thing with our marriage, watching the replay, just running the same plays, never looking up to see if the game has changed."

Claire had stared at him. In twenty-six years, Greg had never once used a sports metaphor to describe their relationship. It wasn't poetry, but it was Greg, and Greg was trying to articulate his inner life through baseball, which was actually the most romantic thing he'd done in many years.

"The game has changed," Claire said.

"Yeah," Greg said, smiling slightly. "I'm starting to see that."

Then they had driven home separately, as they always did after therapy. Claire needed those twenty minutes in the car alone to process what had happened. She thought Greg probably did, too.

When she got home, Greg was in the kitchen, not in the den. He was standing at the stove, looking confused. The air smelled like burning garlic or something that he might have been attempting to stir-fry.

"What are you doing?" Claire asked.

"Cooking," Greg said. He was holding a spatula, but had a look on his face as if he had only held one, maybe three times in his life.

"The garlic is burning."

"I know. How do I make it stop burning?"

"Well, the first thing would be to turn the heat down."

He turned the heat down, but the garlic kept smoking.

Greg stared at the pan, then looked at Claire,

then back at the pan. And then his face did something she hadn't seen in decades, decades. He looked actually sheepish, but endearingly so, like a man who had just discovered that cooking was harder than it looked and was very embarrassed to be discovering it at 52 years old.

"I watched a video," he said, "on my phone. It said stir-fry was easy."

"Who said stir-fry was easy?"

"I don't know, a man on YouTube who had a very convincing voice."

Claire looked at the stove. The garlic was basically charcoal. The chicken was completely raw, and the vegetables were sitting on the counter in a bag, still uncut. The rice cooker wasn't plugged in. It was, by every measurable standard, a complete disaster.

She started laughing. It wasn't the polite laugh that she'd perfected over years of parent-teacher conferences or the careful laugh she used when Greg said something that wasn't funny but needed to be acknowledged. It was a real laugh from her belly, the kind that made her bend over and made her eyes water, because here was her husband, who hadn't cooked a meal in their twenty-six-year marriage, standing at the stove with burnt garlic and a YouTube education and a baffled expression of a man who had decided at least to try.

"Hey, I'm trying here!"

She waved her hand as she bent over, laughing. "I know. I'm so sorry! I just can't stop laughing…"

He watched her laugh, and then he started laughing, too.

The kitchen smelled terrible, the stir-fry was ruined, and neither of them seemed to care because they were in the kitchen laughing together for the first time in longer than either of them could remember.

"Pizza?" Claire said, wiping her eyes.

"Pizza," Greg agreed.

They ordered pizza and ate it at the kitchen table, not in the den, and Greg asked her about the painting class she had coming up. Claire told him, and he had listened. He didn't check his phone. He didn't look toward the den. He sat across from her, ate pizza, and listened to his wife talk about watercolors.

It wasn't perfect or easy, but it was the best dinner they'd had in years.

Harper brought Jordan to Beaufort on a Saturday afternoon. Claire had been preparing for this the way she prepared for everything, very thoroughly. She'd cleaned the house, made Greg promise to wear a shirt that actually had buttons, and baked a pound cake, because pound cake was her answer to every occasion. There was no reason to stop now.

Nina drove from Edisto with a bottle of wine and Elena's empanadas, which Elena had insisted on contributing, because Elena was incapable of allowing a social gathering to occur without her food being present.

Jordan arrived driving Harper's vehicle, which was a big deal because Harper never let anyone else drive, and she had apparently decided that she could ride shotgun as long as Jordan was the person driving the car. He unfolded himself from the car because he was tall. He had broad shoulders, brown hair with some gray at the temples. His face was handsome. He wore jeans and a blue button-down, with his sleeves rolled up to his forearms, and the kind of tan that came from working outside.

He shook Claire's hand on the porch. His grip was warm and firm, and he looked her in the eye, which was a plus for Claire.

"Claire, I've heard so much about you that I feel like I should apologize for how long it took me to get here."

"Well, that's all Harper's fault," Claire said.

"It is entirely Harper's fault," he agreed, a quirk of a smile on his face as Harper stood behind him rolling her eyes.

Greg emerged from the house, as promised, wearing a buttoned shirt, and shook Jordan's hand.

"You build furniture?" he said.

Within fifteen minutes, they were on the back porch talking about wood grain. Claire watched Greg lean forward in his chair with the kind of interest she hadn't seen from him in years outside of a Braves game. She thought to herself, *there you are. I forgot you could do that.*

Then Nina arrived, and the evening started to take shape. The porch, the wine, and the empanadas that disappeared in twelve minutes because Elena's empanadas were addictive.

Jordan fit into their group like a missing piece fits into a puzzle. He was easy. He laughed at the right moments and listened at the right moments. He told a story about the time Harper locked her keys in the car outside his workshop and then refused to call AAA because she was convinced she could break into her own vehicle using a YouTube tutorial. Turned out she could not, and Jordan had to cut a spare key from the one she had given him two years earlier.

"You kept my key?" Harper said. She was genuinely surprised.

"I kept everything," Jordan said.

Harper looked at him. Claire saw it happen. It was the moment Harper let something go. Not everything, of course, not all at once, but a little piece of her wall came down visibly right there in front of everyone.

Harper leaned into Jordan's shoulder, and Nina caught Claire's eye across the porch. The look between them lasted only a split second, but contained thirty years of friendship, and the joy of watching someone you love finally stop running from happiness.

Greg returned from the kitchen with more wine and sat next to Claire. His knee brushed against hers, and neither of them moved away. That simple touch, so common yet profoundly meaningful, made Claire look away to hide her tears from others. They were sharing a moment at a dinner party naturally, without any prompting or therapy. Greg's knee against hers, a seemingly trivial act of closeness, affected her deeply.

Nina called at ten o'clock the next morning. Claire was on the porch with her coffee, watching the river flow by, which was what she did on Sunday mornings now instead of cleaning. Greg was inside making them breakfast. He was doing it more often, the cooking, and the results were improving. They'd gone from disaster to edible. And last Thursday, he made something that could legitimately be described as good, although Claire would never tell him because she didn't need to tell him it was good. The look on his face when he plated the eggs was the look of a man who already knew.

"I need to tell you something," Nina said.

"Good something or bad something?"

"I don't know yet. Both, maybe."

She paused for a long moment.

"Sam came over last night for dinner. He met Lucia officially."

Claire set her coffee down.

"How did it go?"

"He brought her flowers, like separate from mine, a little bouquet with daisies and a card that said nice to meet you. It didn't feel like he was trying too hard or trying to be David. He was just being himself."

"And Lucia?"

"Well, Lucia was Lucia. She asked him six questions in the first ten minutes, including what his stance was on climate change and whether he thought pineapple belonged on pizza. He answered all of them. He said he was against pineapple on pizza, but he respected those who disagreed, which Lucia said was the correct and diplomatic response."

Claire smiled. She could picture it. Lucia at the kitchen table, David's eyes sharp in evaluating, Sam sitting across from her with his kind face, being interviewed by a sixteen-year-old who had the intensity of someone interviewing him at a congressional hearing.

"So did she like him?"

"She said, and I'm quoting, 'He's not weird. His shoes were clean, and he didn't talk about himself the whole time.'"

"Well, that's high praise from Lucia."

"That's the highest praise Lucia has ever given anyone since her eighth-grade English teacher, and she still sends that woman Christmas cards." Nina was quiet for a moment. "But here's the part I need to tell you. After Sam left, Lucia went to her room. I thought she was fine. I mean, she seemed fine. Then I walked past her door, and I heard her crying."

Claire's chest tightened.

"I knocked," Nina said. "She didn't answer. I opened the door. She's sitting on the bed holding her photo of her and David from the mantle. You know, the one from the beach where she's on his shoulders and they're both laughing hysterically."

Claire knew the photo. She had seen it every time she visited Nina's house. David in board shorts, Lucia, tiny and grinning, the Atlantic surf behind them.

"I sat next to her," Nina said, "and she said, 'I like him, Mom. That's why I'm crying, because I liked him. And I feel like he's replacing Dad. And I know that's not what's happening, but it felt like it.'"

"So what did you say?" Claire asked.

"I told her the truth, that nobody could ever replace her dad, that Dad is permanent. He's in her eyes, and he's in Elena's cooking and in that mole recipe and in the boots sitting by the back door. And that liking Sam doesn't mean that she's losing Dad. It means she's got room for more people, and Dad would have wanted her to have the room."

"What did she say?"

"She said, 'Okay.' Then she said, 'Can he come back for dinner next week? I'd like to ask him about his garden.'"

Claire laughed. "She's incredible, Nina. She's David's kid through and through."

Nina paused for a moment.

"Elena met him too, last week. I didn't tell you

because I was waiting to see if Elena would say something awful."

"And did she?"

"She made him sit in her kitchen for an hour and a half. She fed him three courses, asked about his mother, his church attendance, and whether he knew how to change a tire. Then she walked him to the door and said, in English, because she wanted to make sure he understood, 'You are not my son, but you are kind to his wife, and that is enough.'"

Claire pressed her hand over her mouth.

"Then she called me an hour later," Nina said, "told me his table manners were acceptable, but his haircut needed work. And would I please tell him that Elena knows a good barber?"

They laughed. They laughed the way they always did when Elena was involved, because she said things with love, but it was always hard to predict or contain the force of nature that was Elena.

Greg appeared on the porch behind Claire, holding a plate with two scrambled eggs, a piece of toast, and a small glass of orange juice. He set it on the table next to her coffee and said, "Breakfast," and then went back inside.

Nina heard it through the phone.

"Was that Greg?"

"That was Greg bringing me breakfast, unprompted."

"How are the eggs?"

Claire looked at the plate. The eggs were slightly overcooked. The toast was a shade past golden, and the orange juice was in a wine glass because Greg apparently couldn't find a regular glass or didn't even think to look.

"They're perfect," Claire said.

CHAPTER 16

Claire hadn't held a paintbrush in twenty-seven years, and the first thing she did with one was drop it. It slipped right out of her fingers and landed on the drop cloth with a loud, wet slap, leaving a streak of blue across the canvas of the woman standing next to her. This was not the impression Claire had been hoping to make within the first ninety seconds of a painting class.

The woman, who was a retired dentist named Phyllis, had signed up because her therapist told her she needed a creative outlet. She looked at the blue streak on her canvas.

"Well, I was going to paint a sunset. I guess I'll have a river now. I guess I can work with that."

Claire apologized four times. Phyllis told her to

stop apologizing and start painting, advice Claire needed in several areas of her life.

The class was at a studio in downtown Beaufort, a bright converted warehouse space with exposed brick and tall windows. The instructor was a woman named Marianna, who wore paint-splattered overalls and talked about color the way most people speak about religion. She had wiry, unruly brown hair with streaks of gray in it and looked like she'd probably been living in a commune at some point.

She had set up twelve easels in a loose semicircle, each with a blank canvas and a set of acrylics. There was also a jar of water and a collection of brushes in various sizes. The whole arrangement looked inviting and terrifying.

Most people wouldn't think a painting class was a big adventure, but she'd chosen it because she'd been sketching since karaoke night, filling her notebook with waves, marshes, and the view from her porch at sunrise. The sketching had awakened something buried so deep that she'd almost forgotten it was even there.

She used to paint in college, before Greg, before the kids, before a third-grade classroom and pantry organization had overtaken her life. Before twenty-six years of making everything beautiful for everyone else but herself. She used to stay in the art building at the College of Charleston until two o'clock in the morning, smelling of turpentine and paint.

And they weren't that great, but they came from a place inside her that didn't have any countdown or to-do list.

She stopped painting when it got practical, which was another way of saying she'd stopped painting when she got scared. Scared that it wouldn't lead anywhere, scared that she wasn't good enough, scared that wanting something just for herself would come off as selfish, because the world had told Claire Morrison that a good woman was a useful woman, and painting was not really useful.

Painting was indulgent. It was the kind of thing you did before you had responsibilities. But once responsibilities arrived, painting went into a closet, and that closet got smaller and smaller until you forgot there was even a door.

Harper was at the easel to Claire's left. She was looking at her brushes with an intensity as if she were evaluating all the proper tools for the job. She'd arranged them by size, of course. Nina was to Claire's right, running her fingers over the canvas.

"Okay, everyone," Marianna said, clapping to bring the room to attention. She had the energy of someone who had drunk six espressos that morning.

"Today is not about technique. It's about making something pretty. It's about making something honest. I just want you to paint what you feel, not what you see or what you think. I want what's actually happening inside of you right now, in this room, on this day."

"What if what I feel is just confused?" asked a man who looked like he had probably been dragged there by his wife.

"Then paint confused," Marianna said. "Confused has a color. It might actually have several."

Harper leaned toward Claire. "What color is confused? I think maybe I'm confused."

"For you, probably the color of a spreadsheet that doesn't balance."

"Ooh, that's red."

"Confused is definitely red then."

"Start there," Marianna said, because she had heard them. "Start with whatever shows up first. You can always paint over it later."

Claire picked up a brush, a new one, not the one she'd dropped. She dipped it in the blue, the color of the accidental river on Phyllis's canvas, and touched it to the white surface.

The mark was small, a single curved line. Could have been a wave or a road or the beginning of something she hadn't named yet.

And then she made another mark and another mark. The brush moved, and Claire's brain suddenly shut up for the first time in a long time because painting was the one thing that had always done this for her. Silenced the inner organizer, the woman who counted to three.

Painting operated on a different frequency. And Claire had forgotten how much she needed that frequency.

Harper, of course, approached painting the same way she approached everything in her life: with immense strategy. She looked at her canvas for a whole three minutes before even touching it. Then she picked out two brushes, a medium and a fine, and laid out four colors as if she were planning a quarterly report. Then she began to paint, and what emerged was architectural, sharp lines, geometric shapes, precise. It looked like a blueprint for a building that hadn't been built yet, and it was actually good. Harper had an eye for structure, but it was also what Claire expected, because Harper's painting looked like Harper, organized, impressive, and completely contained.

Until it wasn't.

Marianna had been circling the room, stopping at each easel, offering her observations quietly. When she reached Harper, she stood there for a long moment, tilting her head.

"You're thinking too much," Marianna said.

"Well, I'm a thinker," Harper said. "It's what I do. It's my primary function."

"No, your primary function right now is to paint, not plan a painting. There's a difference." Marianna picked up a wide brush, dipped it in a warm orange color, and handed it to Harper. "Do something with this that you can't take back."

Harper stared at the brush, then at her canvas. Then at Marianna, who waited with patience.

Harper dragged the orange brush in a long, uncontrolled stroke across the center of her painting, right through all the geometric shapes. And somewhere in the middle of it, she made a sound that was either a gasp or a laugh.

"No," Marianna said, "keep going."

So Harper kept going. She added yellow and then red. She layered color over architecture until the sharp lines were visible underneath, but no longer the dominant part of the painting.

The painting was messy and imperfect, and it was probably the most interesting thing Harper had produced in a long time.

She stood in front of the painting with paint on her silk blouse that she had again worn to a painting class because she was Harper, and her expression was that of a woman who had just discovered something about herself that she didn't quite understand.

"I ruined it," she said.

"You started it," Marianna said. "The ruining is where art begins."

Claire looked at Harper's painting and thought about Jordan's workshop and the table he was building for her with reclaimed church wood. Harper was a woman being slowly, carefully taken apart and reassembled by a man with patient hands and a spare key that he'd kept for four years. The painting looked like what that probably felt like, structure giving way to warmth.

Nina painted a marsh scene, because of course she did. She painted it from the angle of the kitchen window on Edisto at sunrise, the view that David had fallen in love with, the view that she saw every morning when she made her one cup of coffee. She worked slowly, mixing the colors with the same patience she'd learned at Señora Morales's stove. She didn't paint David, she didn't paint the boots by the door, or any of the other artifacts of his presence. She painted the view he loved in his honor. The painting was basically of David without David, and it was beautiful in the way loss sometimes is.

Marianna stopped at Nina's easel and didn't say anything for a moment.

"Who taught you that? Who taught you to see light like that?" she said.

"My husband. He used to photograph this view almost every morning. He said the light was different every day and it was never wrong."

"He was correct," Marianna said. "The light is never wrong."

Nina painted for two hours without stopping. She barely spoke. She didn't even look at anyone else's canvas. She just stood there in front of her easel and moved the brush, and the marsh appeared inch by inch.

Finally, she stepped back and looked at the whole thing, pressed her hand over her mouth, and stood still.

Claire watched her from one easel away and recognized that expression. It was the same face Nina had made when she tasted the mole, the same face she'd made reading her letter at the grief retreat. It was a woman encountering something she had made, something that had come from within her, and finding that the outside version was true.

"It really looks like home," Nina said.

"It is home," Claire said.

Claire's painting was the most time-consuming, and she initially thought it made the least sense, but she loved it. She began with a beautiful blue, and the waves transformed into something abstract - not water or any clear image - just layers of color: blue, green, and gold. A deep rose hue, almost the same as her fridge napkin, blended into the colors without strict boundaries, and the shapes were loose. If she tilted her head and squinted, she might see a woman, a porch over-looking water, or a doorway - but she might not see anything at all. Claire didn't care. This realization was profound. She'd spent 27 years avoiding painting for fear it wouldn't be good enough, yet now she stood before a messy, abstract canvas - something unlikely to be displayed in a gallery to impress anyone - but she didn't care. This painting was for herself. It was the first piece she'd created in years that existed purely because she wanted it to.

Marianna came to her easel last. She stood

behind Claire, looking at the painting for a long time. Claire had been through this before in college, so she braced herself for the critique, for some suggestion about her composition or color theory.

"This is brave," Marianna said.

Claire blinked. "It's actually just a big mess."

"It's abstract, and it's honest. It came from somewhere real inside of you, and that is not a mess. That's called art." Marianna tilted her head. "How long since you've painted?"

"About twenty-seven years."

"Well, then, this is a homecoming. Welcome back."

Claire looked at her canvas again. The dusty rose color was right there in the center, surrounded by blues and golds. It looked like nothing and everything at the same time. She stood there in front of it and felt something she hadn't felt since all those years ago in the art building at the College of Charleston at two in the morning. The pure joy of making something that didn't need to justify its existence.

Oh, gosh, she was crying. Not the controlled tears she'd perfected for sad movies, but real tears that came when something locked opened up. She wiped her eyes with the back of her hand, got paint on her face, and then just didn't wipe it off.

"You know you have paint on your face," Harper said.

"I know."

"Well, are you gonna wipe it off?"

"No."

Harper looked at her. She dipped her finger in the orange from her own canvas and drew a streak on her cheekbone. "There, now we match."

Nina looked at both of them. She picked up her brush and loaded it with gold from her marsh sunrise and then painted a stripe across the bridge of her nose. "War paint," she said.

Phyllis, the retired dentist, looked at the three of them from behind her accidental river canvas. "Y'all are my kind of people."

The room started laughing, and Marianna shook her head and smiled.

Claire stood between her two best friends with blue all over her face and a painting on the easel that she was going to take home and hang on the wall of her guest room. She realized it wasn't a guest room at all anymore. It was becoming hers, a room of her own, a place that she had claimed not as a refuge from her marriage, but as a declaration of herself, a place where her sketchbooks lived and her paintings would hang.

She would tell Greg about it tonight. She would say, "I want to keep the guest room as my studio."

He would say, "Okay," because Greg was learning to say okay to things he didn't fully understand.

She would show him the painting, and he might get it, and he might not.

And either was fine.

They all cleaned up together, washed their brushes, and carefully carried their wet canvases to Claire's car. They loaded the trunk, arranging the paintings so they wouldn't touch.

"Your painting is touching my painting," Harper said.

"They're wet. They're going to touch."

"My painting doesn't want to be touched."

"Your painting is abstract chaos, Harper. It can handle contact," Claire said.

Nina placed hers carefully in the back seat, propped up against the headrest like a passenger. "I'm going to give this to Elena," she said.

"Really?" Claire asked, looking at her.

"It's the view from the kitchen, the view David loved. Elena's never had a painting of it. She has photos, of course, but not a painting." Nina touched the window. "She'll pretend she doesn't like it. She'll say something about how the egrets look too thin, or the water is the wrong shade of silver, and then she'll hang it in her kitchen and never take it down."

Claire thought about Elena, five feet of fury and love, hanging Nina's painting in her kitchen next to the saints and the photos of David. She thought about the thread that connected all of them. Every act of love in this story passed through food or art, the mole, the index cards, the food, and now the painting. All of those things, whether food or art, said the same: *I made this with my hands, and it's for you. It carries the memory of everyone who made it before me.*

"One more," Claire said, looking at her friends across the car. "One more adventure."

"Yeah, the big one," Harper said.

"Skydiving," Nina said.

They stood in the parking lot with paint on their faces, and the word skydiving hung in the air between them.

"Are we really ready for something like that?" Claire asked.

"Nope, not in the slightest," Harper said.

"Yeah, absolutely not. I'm gonna say we are definitely not ready," Nina said.

"Good," Claire said. "That's the whole point of all

of this."

CHAPTER 17

Claire's kitchen smelled like mole. Not like Señora Morales's mole, but Nina's mole. Nina's version, that she'd learned from the index cards and practiced over and over in her kitchen on Edisto until Elena tasted it and said, "It's not David's, it's yours, and that's better." That was the highest compliment Elena had ever given that didn't involve criticizing someone's haircut in the same sentence.

Nina had brought the ingredients in two grocery bags and taken them over to Claire's kitchen. And now she stood at the stove, toasting chilies on Claire's comal, which Claire didn't even own eleven months ago. She had bought one after cooking class because some things, once they enter your life, just refuse to leave.

Harper was on chili soaking duty, which meant

she was just standing at the counter with a bowl of hot water and a timer on her phone.

"The recipe says fifteen minutes," she said. "It has been eleven. I will report when we reach fifteen."

"You know the chilies don't care a thing about your timer, Harper," Nina said.

"The chilies are soaking in water. They are subject to the law of physics, just like everything else."

"Señora Morales said the chilies are done when they're done, not when a phone tells them to be."

"Well, Señora Morales is a culinary genius, I will admit that, but I'm a woman with a spreadsheet and a timer, and we have to work with what we have."

Claire was chopping tomatoes. She was not good at chopping tomatoes, and she knew this. She mainly squished them instead of chopping them, but she didn't care. She'd been practicing that sentence in various forms for almost a year now. She didn't care. She just had to wait until she actually felt it.

She chopped the tomatoes unevenly, and they went into the roasting pan unevenly, but the mole would be no worse for it.

Tomorrow, they were all jumping out of an airplane.

The thought kept arriving uninvited, like a guest who shows up early and gets in your way the entire time you're trying to prepare for a party. It just stood in the corner of every conversation, every laugh, every moment, waiting to be looked at and acknowledged.

Tomorrow morning at nine o'clock, the three of them were going to drive to a small airfield outside of Beaufort, climb into a perfectly good plane, ascend to 14,000 feet, and then voluntarily, like three nutcases, on purpose, step out of the good airplane.

Claire had not told Greg any of the specifics. She just told him they were doing their last adventure tomorrow, and she'd be home by the afternoon. At least she prayed she would be home by the afternoon.

He had asked, for the first time in their marriage, "Well, what is it?"

And she had said, "Skydiving."

He looked at her with an expression she'd never seen on his face before. Fear.

It wasn't a confused concern or anything that looked distant. It wasn't the man who had said "have fun" for six months without asking any questions. She saw real fear, the fear of a man who had just realized that his wife was about to throw herself out of an airplane, and he was not ready to lose her.

"Be very careful," he said.

He said it while holding her hands, which he

hadn't done in the kitchen since their anniversary fifteen years ago. His eyes were actually a little wet.

Claire understood that his way of saying "be careful" was Greg's way of saying, *I love you, and I'm scared, and I'm only understanding right now what it would mean to lose you.*

She kissed him on the cheek. "I'll be careful."

"Promise me."

"I promise."

It was the most honest exchange they'd had outside of the doctor's office, and it had happened over a cutting board, which seemed right, because the best conversations in a home always happened in the kitchen.

The mole took three hours to cook, and those three hours were the best part. It wasn't the mole itself, although it was very good and rich and dark. The whole house smelled like someone's grandmother's kitchen. But the best part was the making of it. Nina at the stove, directing everyone. Harper at the counter, grinding spices in the molca-jete that Nina brought because Claire's spice grinder, according to Nina, was "a machine designed to remove the soul from cumin." Claire was roasting tomatillos under the broiler, watching the skins blister and char.

They talked while they cooked, but not about tomorrow, about everything else, about the whole year.

"Oh my gosh, do you remember the karaoke?" Claire said, laughing. "At Hank's? I swear, Nina, you almost didn't get out of the car."

"I almost didn't get out of the car for many of them," Nina said. "That was kind of my thing back then."

"Yeah, your thing was getting out of the car anyway," Harper said. "That was the brave part. Not the adventure at first. It was the car door."

Nina stirred the mole. The chocolate was now going in, two tablets, dark and grainy, dissolving into the sauce. This time, Nina's hands weren't shaking as they had been at Señora Morales's house. Now she stirred with a steady rhythm of a woman who had made this recipe at least five times.

"Oh, and the polar plunge," Nina said. "Claire, you screamed so loud a jogger stopped to make sure nobody was drowning."

"Well, that water was thirty-seven degrees. I think screaming was completely appropriate."

"And the matching bathing suits," Harper said.

"Navy with polka dots. I can't believe you bought us matching bathing suits, Claire."

"I told you they were on sale. It was a really good sale."

"They were coordinated. You coordinated our polar plunge like we were triplets."

"Well, someone has to maintain standards around here."

Harper opened a bottle of wine while the mole simmered. She poured three glasses, and they moved to the kitchen table.

Claire's phone was open to a folder of the photos from the past eleven months. They scrolled through them together, leaning in, their heads almost touching.

The karaoke stage at Hank's, blurry and dark, their three shapes in the spotlight.

The polar plunge, taken by the jogger who had stopped to watch, the three of them in polka dots, waist-deep, mouths hanging open in shock.

Nina at Señora Morales's stove, stirring, tears running down her face.

The tattoo parlor in Savannah, with Wren bent over Harper's wrist.

The diner outside Hendersonville, three glasses of sweet tea and that big basket of biscuits.

The hotel room in Asheville, Claire on the

pullout couch, sketching, while Nina smiled at the ceiling.

Their speed dating name tags, lined up in a row.

The grief retreat, a photo Nina had asked Claire to take of the rocking chairs on the porch.

Hank's sign, Folly Beach at dawn, their wave tattoos.

Harper's comedy face, mouth open, finger pointing at the audience.

Clementine the horse, her nose against Nina's shoulder.

Claire's painting on an easel, war paint on their faces.

Eleven months, eleven adventures, some of them not a big deal to other people, but very big deals to them. These three women, who had sat on a porch a year ago and admitted the truth, signed a napkin, and then just jumped.

"Who were we?" Harper said, scrolling back to the beginning.

There was a photo of them from the birthday dinner that Claire had taken at the table, with three of them raising their glasses. The difference in that photo and the ones that came after was so visible that it made Claire's chest clench.

In the birthday photo, they were smiling. In the later photos, they were alive.

There was a real difference.

"We were so scared," Nina said.

"I think we're still scared," Claire said. "I mean, we're jumping out of an airplane tomorrow."

"Yeah, but it's a different kind of scared," Nina said.

She was looking at the birthday photo of the woman who had been so different all those months ago, wearing David's sweater like armor.

"Back then, I was just scared of living. Now I'm scared of an airplane."

"I think that's a legitimate fear."

Harper laughed, then Claire, and then they were all laughing.

As Claire smelled the mole and looked at the photos, she thought, *This is what a year of bravery looks like. It's not a highlight reel. It's a kitchen full of food and laughter, and the people who showed up over and over.*

They ate at the table that Greg had cleared for them before he left for his brother's house for the night. He had cleared the table without being asked. He'd moved his laptop, his earbuds, and the stack of mail that had been sitting there accumulating for the last week. He'd put out the good plates, the ones Claire used for birthdays and Thanksgiving. He'd even left a note on the counter that said, *"Have fun tonight. I'll be thinking about you tomorrow. Be brave. Love, G."*

Claire had read the note three times and then put it in the drawer with her sketchbooks. That's where she kept things that mattered.

The mole was delicious, rich, dark, and smoky, layered in a way that felt like tasting the whole history of a country in a single spoonful. Nina served it over rice the way David did, and they ate at Claire's table with those good plates and the wine.

"Elena would approve," Harper said.

"No, Elena would say that this rice is over-cooked," Nina said.

"Is the rice overcooked?"

"Slightly. Don't tell Elena."

After dinner, they moved to the dining room with the wine. Claire had put blankets on the floor with pillows, creating what looked like a nest. It was comfortable and slightly absurd, but they sank into it and didn't get up.

The napkin was on the coffee table. Claire had taken it off the fridge for the first time all year and put it next to the wine, next to some of the photos they'd printed at the drugstore that afternoon on an impulse.

It looked different from what it had been eleven months ago. The dusty rose had faded to a softer hue. The ink had blurred at the edges. Harper's sharp handwriting was still legible.

The pact. Three rules, three signatures underneath.

Nina picked it up. She held it carefully. "We did it," she said. "Just one big adventure left."

"Yep, we did do it," Claire said.

"We did it because of you," Harper said to Nina. "You said yes first on that porch. You held out your hand and said, give me the pen. If you hadn't done that, then that thing would probably still be blank."

Nina looked at the napkin. She traced her signature with her finger. Then she traced Claire's and Harper's.

"David is everywhere on this napkin," she said. "He's in so many of the things I did this year. The mole, of course. But also the tattoo and the cooking class. I signed that napkin because David would have told me to. So every adventure I went on, I did because of him. And every adventure changed me into someone who isn't only about him anymore. Sometimes that part makes me cry. That he gave me this, and this gave me something different. His memory gave me freedom."

The room was quiet. Outside, the Beaufort night breathed, warm and slow.

Harper put her hand on Nina's knee. She didn't say anything. Harper had learned over the months of grief and growth that the bravest thing you could sometimes do was not speak.

Claire reached over and put her hand on Nina's other knee. And the three of them sat in the living room in their nest of blankets and pillows.

"I need to say something," Claire said.

"You always need to say something," Harper said, rolling her eyes. "It's part of your charm."

"I need to say that this year saved me. Not the adventures, but both of you. I was disappearing inside my own life, and you both pulled me out. You didn't try to fix me. You just stood next to me while I fixed myself. I spent twenty-six years making everything beautiful for other people, and this year I made something beautiful for me. And you were there the whole time."

"We were there because you built the table," Nina said. "Literally. You set this table. You made the dinner. You changed the napkin color four times. If you hadn't made that birthday dinner perfect, we wouldn't have ended up on the porch. And the porch is where everything started."

"Those napkins were a very aggressive salmon," Harper said.

"They were dusty rose. The original choice was salmon."

"You told us it looked like the cafeteria."

"The *original* original choice was coral, which also looked like salmon."

"Different salmon."

"The coral was sophisticated salmon, and the second one was hospital salmon."

"Claire, all salmon is the same salmon."

"That is terribly false, and I will die on that hill."

Nina was laughing, lying on the blankets with a wine glass balanced on her stomach. She was laughing about an argument over the color of salmon and the particular insanity Claire had of caring so deeply about napkin colors that she had to change them four times. The napkin story was something she could listen to over and over, although it didn't really matter in the grand scheme of things. But it did matter. The napkins mattered. All those details mattered.

Claire's obsessive, meticulous, beautiful attention to little things was not a flaw. It was a gift. It was the same gift that had made that birthday dinner so perfect and the karaoke song list so organized. It was the gift that gave them matching bathing suits. Claire Morrison noticed things that other people walked right past. She made them beautiful, and the world was better for it.

The wine ran out. They didn't open another bottle. They just lay on the floor of Claire's living room, three women on the eve of their last adventure.

"Are you scared?" Claire said. "About tomorrow?"

"Terrified," Harper said.

"Yeah, completely and totally terrified," Nina replied.

"Good," Claire said. "That's the whole point of all of this, right? To finish by doing one of the scariest things we can imagine? To prove that we're different now?"

"I just hope we're not three flat pancakes by lunchtime," Harper said, closing her eyes and pretending to pray.

Surprisingly, they all fell asleep on the floor. Not all at once, of course. Nina first, because Nina always fell asleep first. Claire second, her sketchbook open on the blanket next to her, a pencil still dangling in her hand. Harper last, because Harper was always last. She was the one who always kept watch, always made sure everyone else was safe before she allowed herself to close her eyes.

The house settled around them. The candles burned low and went out. Crickets and frogs made sounds in the distance. The napkin sat on the coffee table in the dark, faded and worn.

Tomorrow, they would carry it to the airfield, put it in one of their pockets, and jump.

And whatever happened after that would be their next thing, and then the next thing after that, because the pact had never really been about just twelve adventures. It had been about learning to say yes, and they had all learned that lesson very well.

They didn't need courage anymore.

In the morning, the sun would come up over the marsh, and those three women would wake up, stiff and sore from sleeping on the living room floor. They would drink too much coffee.

They would drive to an airfield, hands shaking, and step out of an airplane. The world would be bigger from up there than any of them could imagine, but that was tomorrow. Tonight, they slept, together on the floor like they were at a middle school slumber party, the way that they used to sleep in their dorm at the College of Charleston, tangled up in comfy blankets, safe in each other's company, dreaming about whatever comes next.

The plane was yellow, but not a comforting shade. It wasn't like school bus yellow or the bright yellow of a sunny day. It certainly wasn't the cheerful, vintage kitchen wall yellow from the '70s. Instead, it was a color that seemed to say, 'I was painted this way so you can spot me in a field if something goes wrong.' The small plane looked loud and neglected, sitting on the Skydive Lowcountry tarmac like a toy left outside too long. It would carry them 14,000 feet into the sky, and then, like some fools, they would just jump right out.

Nina stood on the tarmac, looking at the plane. "We have done karaoke, polar plunges, cooking classes, rock climbing, tattoos, road trips, speed dating, grief retreats, stand-up comedy, and horseback riding. We've signed a napkin and kept our word to each other. And now this small yellow machine is going to take us up, and we are willingly going to jump to our deaths."

The napkin was in her pocket. She had taken it from Claire's coffee table that morning, folded it carefully, and put it in the breast pocket of the jumpsuit they had given her at check-in. The jumpsuit was neon green so she could be found in a field if something went wrong. It was very important to have visibility after a disaster. Claire's was orange and Harper's was blue.

The morning had started at Claire's house with way too much coffee and not enough breakfast. They had all woken up on the living room floor, stiff-backed, as expected. The aching necks were a little much, though. Fifty-year-old women should not sleep on hardwood floors, and they were now remembering why they didn't do it anymore.

Claire had made coffee. Harper had complained about her spine. Nina had eaten a banana, just stared out the window, and thought about David, Sam, Lucia, and Elena. She thought about the letter she'd written at the grief retreat and about the boots that were still at the back door of her cottage. But then she had put on her shoes and gotten into the car.

The drive to the airfield was only twenty minutes from Claire's house. Nobody said a word for the first ten. The Lowcountry slid past. The morning was clear, a sky so blue and deep that it didn't even look real. And they would soon be falling through it.

"I need to say something," Harper said from the backseat. "I am afraid."

Claire looked at her through the rearview mirror. "You're allowed to be afraid."

"I know I'm allowed. I'm just announcing it for the record. Harper Ellis is afraid. I want that documented."

"It has been documented," Nina said.

"Also, if I die, my apartment goes to Jordan. My investment portfolio goes to a scholarship fund I've already set up. And James gets the fiddle-leaf fig. Those are my terms."

"You're not going to die," Claire said.

"Statistically, probably not, but I do like to be prepared for all outcomes."

"Statistically, you're more likely to die driving to the airfield than jumping out of the plane," Nina said.

"And that is not comforting while we are currently driving to the airfield."

The safety briefing took about forty-five minutes and covered everything Nina needed to know, along with several things she now wished she didn't know. Their instructor was a man named Cal. He had a sunburned face and the confidence of someone who had probably jumped out of airplanes about 4,000 times and considered it a perfectly normal way to spend a Tuesday. He was maybe thirty-five, with a lean build and weathered skin.

He walked them through the equipment, the harness, the altimeter, the drogue chute that slowed the free fall, the main canopy, the reserve canopy, which existed in case the main canopy didn't work. And Nina could have gone her whole life without knowing that it existed.

"Tandem jump," Cal said, strapping a harness around Claire's torso. She stood very still with an expression as if she had maybe changed her mind, but just wasn't saying so. "You're attached to me or one of my guys the whole time. We do all the work. You enjoy the ride."

"Define enjoy," Harper said, holding up her finger.

Cal looked at her. "Ma'am, in about thirty minutes, you're gonna be 14,000 feet above the most beautiful coastline in all of America, falling at 120 miles an hour. You're gonna see the curve of the earth. Enjoy means whatever you want it to mean."

Harper blinked slowly. "That's actually not a bad answer."

"Well, I've had practice."

They were assigned to their tandem partners. Claire got Cal. Harper got a woman named Dez, with a shaved head and a tattoo sleeve. She seemed to find the prospect of falling out of the sky genuinely delightful. Nina got a quiet man named Mark, with kind eyes and a very steady demeanor. He looked like he would probably be very calm during the apocalypse.

They walked to the plane. The tarmac was warm under their feet. The sky was impossibly blue, and the airfield was surrounded by the Lowcountry in every direction. On one side, the flat silver line of the Broad River off in the distance. On the other, marshland.

From up there, Nina knew the whole world would be water and green, and the coastline would curve away toward Charleston in one direction and Edisto in the other. Somewhere down there was her house and her kitchen and David's boots sitting by the door.

She touched the napkin in her pocket.

They climbed into the plane. It was smaller than

it looked, all metal and rigging, and smelled of aviation fuel and maybe leftover adrenaline from the last people who were in there. There were no real seats. They sat on a bench along one wall, strapped to their partners. The door was open, which seemed like a very wrong thing for a plane.

The engine roared, the plane taxied, and then the ground fell away.

Claire watched as the earth got smaller and smaller. She was strapped to Cal's chest, facing the open door. The plane was climbing in a long, wide spiral, and through the door she could see the Lowcountry unfolding below her, like a map she'd been living on her whole life but had never seen from above. Rivers, marshes, bridges. She could see the barrier islands, dark green and narrow, strung along the coast like beads on a chain. Beaufort was down there somewhere. Her house, her kitchen. Greg, who was at his brother's house right now, probably looking at his phone, scared, thinking about her for the first time in decades, with the full attention of a man who was terrified of losing something he'd stopped paying attention to.

The altimeter on Cal's wrist read 8,000 feet, then

ten, then twelve. Claire's heart was hammering in her chest, bebopping around, skipping, pumping, beating so hard she could feel it in her teeth. Her hands were shaking. Her breath was fast. She thought about all the things she'd been afraid of in her life and realized that none of them, not a single one, had been as bad as this. Her fear of disappearing, her fear of not mattering, her fear of waking up at fifty and not knowing who she was - those fears were abstract. But this fear, a fear that had an altitude reading and an open door and a very real 14,000-foot gap between herself and the ground, that was real fear.

Cal's voice was in her ear, calm and instructional. "Now, when we get over to that door, I want you to cross your arms over your chest. Lean back into me. I'll do the rest. You just breathe."

"Breathing," Claire said. "I can do breathing. I've been breathing for fifty years."

"Well, there you go."

The plane leveled out. The altimeter read fourteen thousand. The light in the cabin changed. The open door was no longer a rectangle of sky, but an invitation, the last boundary between Claire and who she had been and the Claire she was about to become.

She looked across the cabin at Nina and Harper.

Nina's face was pale, her jaw tight, her hand pressed against her chest. Harper was sitting rigidly upright, attached to Dez, her expression the one she wore in board meetings.

Claire caught Harper's eyes, and Harper caught hers. Across the noise and the wind, they looked at each other, and Claire thought about the porch and the napkin and how they were never going to back out.

Cal walked her to the edge. Claire's feet were at the door, and below her, the earth was impossibly far away. She crossed her arms. She leaned back.

And she fell.

The first second was pure silence. Absolute silence, like the world had taken a deep breath and just held it. Then the wind hit, and the silence became a loud roar.

Claire Morrison was falling through the sky above Beaufort, South Carolina, and she was screaming.

Screaming the way she hadn't screamed in many years. Not a polite, controlled scream, not the kind of scream from a woman who counted to three, but a real, primal scream that came from a deep place, from the unmanaged part of herself.

The Lowcountry spiraled below her. She could see the rivers, threads of green, bridges, marshes, the ocean beyond. She could see the sky above and the earth below, and she was in between, suspended in absolutely nothing, held by nothing except a man named Cal and a harness that she desperately hoped was made well.

And she was being held by the blind, stupid, magnificent trust that the parachute would open and the ground would catch her, that she would survive all of this.

She refused to close her eyes.

The drogue chute deployed. The free fall slowed. Then the main canopy opened with a jolt, snapping her upright.

The roar became a whisper, and now she was floating, floating above her life.

The world below was silent and gorgeous, more beautiful than anything she'd ever seen.

And now she just hung in the sky and laughed.

No screams this time, just a laugh, the laugh of a woman who had just done the most terrifying thing she could imagine.

And on the other side of that terror was not safety, but something even better - a knowledge that she could survive anything, because she just had.

Harper jumped second. She walked to the door with Dez and looked down, and her brain did what her brain always did. It calculated. It ran numbers. It assessed risk and the probability of every possible outcome, then concluded that her body had already reached the conclusion that this was insane.

"Ready?" Dez asked.

"No," Harper said. "Go."

They fell.

The wind took everything. It stole her thoughts and her plans. It took away her quarterly projections and her corner office. It removed her 14th-floor view and her $200 million portfolio, and scattered them into the sky like confetti.

For the first time in her whole life, Harper Ellis was not in control of anything. She could not control the speed, the direction, or the outcome of what was about to happen. She was just a body in the air, subject to physics, the law of gravity, and subject to the terrifying reality that no amount of preparation could change what was happening to her, and that what was happening was that she was falling and that she couldn't stop it.

She was silent.

Dez would later say to her that most people screamed or cried. One man even sang the national anthem, but Harper was silent the entire way down, eyes wide open.

She took in everything: the coastline, the curve of the earth, the blue, and the green. She'd been rushing through this world for fifty years without stopping to look at it, and now she had no choice.

She thought about Jordan and the workshop in Mount Pleasant. She thought about the sawdust on the floor and the table he was building her. She thought about the drawer, the fourth chair, and the coffee he made her with one sugar, and the fact that she was finally letting him do all of those things.

She thought about her mom, her cousin Margaux and her children, the tall divorced surgeon. She thought about the toast over the sink in her apartment with no kitchen table, and all the years she had spent building a life that looked perfect but felt empty.

I'm done with that, she thought to herself. *I'm done with eating while I stand up. I'm done with keeping my options open so I don't have to make hard choices. I choose this. I choose him. I choose the table, the drawer, and the mess of being known by someone who isn't afraid of me.*

The canopy opened, and the world went quiet.

She floated above the Lowcountry, completely still.

This must be what relaxation feels like.

How odd for her to feel it while she was dropping out of a plane.

She was just here, present, a woman in the sky, fifty years old, finally looking at everything with open eyes and an open heart.

This is what it feels like to stop holding your breath.

N ina jumped last.

She jumped last because she had been first many times during the year. First one to sign the napkin, first one to pick an adventure. She was even the first one to walk toward the karaoke stage. She was the first one to cry in cooking class, the first one to read her letter.

And now, at the end of this, she wanted to be the last one to close the door on the year, the last one out of the plane, the last one flying through the air, and the last one to carry the napkin through the sky.

Mark had her strapped to his chest. They waddled over to the door because there was just no graceful way to walk in tandem when you were up at 14,000 feet.

Nina looked down and saw the Lowcountry spread out like the most beautiful painting she'd ever seen. For a moment, she imagined herself going splat right onto that painting, but then she decided to wipe that image from her head because how helpful could it be to imagine yourself going splat in the first place?

She could see the coastline and the islands, and she was pretty sure she could see the dark green shape of Edisto, her island, the place David had looked at from a realtor's kitchen window and said, " This is it. This is where we live."

She pressed her hand against her chest and felt the napkin crinkle under her palm. The three signatures, the three rules they'd made, the twelve months of saying yes to the things that scared them.

"David," she whispered under her breath.

Mark, behind her, couldn't hear. The wind was far too loud, but Nina wasn't saying it for him.

She said it for the sky and for the earth below. She said it for the man who wasn't in either of them anymore, but who was, she had finally learned after all this time, involved in everything she did. In the mole and the karaoke. He was in the freezing ocean. He was in the painting and the letter. And when she looked into Lucia's eyes or Elena's cooking pot, she saw him. When she looked at the wave tattooed on her wrist, she knew he was with her.

David was not gone.

David was the reason she was here, at the door of this yellow airplane, about to free-fall.

And then she jumped.

The fall wasn't what she expected at all.

She'd expected abject terror. She'd braced for it the way she had braced for the karaoke or the grief retreat. She braced for it every time she did anything uncomfortable for the last twelve months.

The terror only lasted for about a second, just that first second, that moment where you step out, and the door disappears, and the plane disappears. The world tilts for a moment.

She was in the air with nothing below her and nothing above her and only a stranger holding onto her.

But after that second, the terror was replaced by something she didn't have a name for. Something bigger than peace, bigger than joy, actually.

It was the feeling of every wall she'd built over the last two years all crumbling down at one time, dissolving.

She felt all of the emotions at once. The love. The grief. The rage. The gratitude.

She had a desperate, aching desire to be alive again, and it all poured out of her at 120 miles per hour in the sky above the Lowcountry of South Carolina.

She wasn't numb anymore. She wasn't living behind glass.

She was falling through the open air with the wind in her face, and now she could feel every single thing.

She could feel David.

But not his ghost. Not even his memory.

His presence.

As warm and close as it was when he stood behind her in the kitchen and wrapped his arms around her waist, when he would put his chin on her shoulder and say, look at that, mi amor, look at that bird.

He was right here.

He was falling with her.

Nina fell through the sky with her dead husband beside her and felt, for one perfect moment, the full weight of being loved by him again and how that would never stop, no matter where he was right now.

Nina floated.

The roar became a whisper. The canopy opened above her. The Lowcountry showed all of its beauty, the rivers, the marshes, the islands, the whole beautiful but heartbreaking world that David had loved.

Nina was choosing that now. She was choosing to love it all in his place.

She could see Beaufort. She could see the bridges and the coast curving south toward Edisto.

And she thought to herself, I am still here.

I am still here, and that is enough.

She floated down, and the ground rose to meet her, slowly, gently, getting closer. As the trees grew taller and the airfield appeared below like an outstretched hand ready to catch her, she landed.

Mark unclipped her and stepped back as her legs buckled and she sat down on the grass. She pressed her hand to the napkin again and looked at the sky that she had just fallen through and wept.

These tears were not from grief. They weren't even the same tears from Señora Morales's kitchen.

These were grateful tears, the tears of a woman who had been dead inside for two years and was now fully alive again, sitting on the ground in her neon green jumpsuit on a Tuesday morning in September.

The sky above her was the same blue it had been when David was alive. And it would be the same blue tomorrow. It would be the same blue forever.

And she was going to be here to see it for as long as she could.

These three women in neon jumpsuits found each other on the field.

They walked across the stretch of grass, still wet with the morning dew, as the yellow plane circled above for the next group of people who had decided to do something insane before lunch.

Claire was crying and laughing at the same time. She'd been doing that since they landed.

Harper was shaking. There was a slight tremor in her hands and jaw, the aftershock of adrenaline working its way through a body that had just been completely out of control for the first time in almost fifty years.

Nina was just sitting on the grass, tear-streaked, makeup running down her face, clutching the napkin in her hand.

They collided with each other, not a hug, but a collision. They came together in a desperate force of people who had just done something extraordinary.

Claire's arms around Nina, Nina's arms around Harper, Harper's arms around both of them, because she was the tallest one with the longest reach.

They held on with a fierceness that would have surprised the women they had been a year ago.

They stood in a knot in the airfield holding each other, and nobody spoke.

Words hadn't even been invented yet for what

they had just done. Not just today, but over the last twelve months.

Claire pulled back first and looked at them. Her mascara was ruined. Her hair was wrecked. She had grass on her jumpsuit and tears rolling down her face.

"We did it," Claire said.

"We did it," Nina said.

"We jumped out of an airplane," Harper said, as if trying to verify a fact that her brain hadn't truly accepted yet.

"Twelve months," Claire said. "We did it. Twelve whole adventures."

"And one napkin," Nina said, holding it up.

The dusty rose was almost white now, the ink barely visible, the edges soft from a year of being touched and read and carried in pockets.

But the words were there. The pact.

Against all odds, these three women who had promised each other they would not back out had kept their promise every single time.

Harper took the napkin from Nina's hand and looked at it. She thought about the night she'd written it, the porch, the frogs, the wine, the moment she'd pulled that pen out from her purse and decided being scared wasn't a reason to stop.

"You know, I think this is the most important

thing I've ever signed," Harper said. "And I've signed contracts worth hundreds of millions of dollars, but none of them ever mattered to me like this."

She handed the napkin to Claire, who folded it carefully and put it in her pocket.

They stood in the airfield.

The plane came in for a landing, yellow against the blue sky, and a new group of people in neon jumpsuits walked toward it, their faces filled with terror.

"You'll be okay!" Harper yelled. "Most likely."

The Lowcountry stretched out around them in every direction. And it was the most beautiful place any of them had ever lived.

They had survived.

And yet they were just getting started.

CHAPTER 19

Nina didn't change the napkin color even once. Unlike Claire, she didn't even think about it. She bought white napkins from the Piggly Wiggly, the kind that came in a plastic pack of 200 for about 4 bucks. She set them on the kitchen table in a pile, not fanned out or folded. They were white, they were napkins, and they were perfectly fine.

Claire would have had feelings about this.

A year ago, Claire would have shown up three hours early and reorganized the entire table with Mason jars and twine. She would have brought dahlia stems in colors complementing the season. But Claire was not hosting this party. Nina was, and Nina's version of hosting was this.

There would be food. There would be people.

Nobody would have an assigned seat, and if you needed a fork, you could open the drawer and get one yourself.

The food was Elena's, all of it.

Elena had arrived at eight in the morning with the Honda rattling and a trunk full of food. She had an expression that suggested she had been cooking before the sun came up, which she had, most likely, because Elena didn't believe in doing things halfway. And she especially didn't believe in doing things halfway when the occasion was her daughter-in-law's birthday.

Pollo asado, frijoles refritos, plátanos fritos, and empanadas that she guarded on the counter as if someone was trying to break in and steal them. Of course, if Harper got there, they would cease to exist within a few minutes. She made flan, a recipe she had been making since before David was born, from a card in her mother's handwriting that was so old the edges were brown.

And, of course, the mole. Not Nina's mole, but Elena's mole, the very original one, the one David had grown up eating.

"You always make way too much food," Nina said, putting her hands on her hips and looking across the counter.

"There's no such thing as too much food. There is only not enough people," Elena said.

She wiped her hands on her apron and looked at Nina, checking her for weight, color, and signs of life. Whatever she saw apparently satisfied her because she nodded once.

"You look good."

"Thank you, Elena."

"The man is coming?"

"Sam?"

"Yes."

"Sam is coming."

"I will behave, don't worry."

"Elena…"

"I said I will behave. I did not say I will not have opinions or thoughts to share with him."

Lucia appeared from her room in a dress that was far too old for her because she was now seventeen, and that's what seventeen-year-olds did. Her dark hair was down, and she was carrying a laptop.

"The slideshow is ready," she announced.

"What slideshow?" Nina asked.

"The slideshow of the pact, all those photos from the year. I put it all to music."

"What music?"

Lucia smiled.

"You'll see."

"Lucia—"

"You'll see, Mom."

They arrived in waves, Claire and Greg first, which didn't surprise anybody because Claire was constitutionally incapable of being late. Greg had apparently decided in this new chapter of their marriage that showing up on time was his only option.

He was wearing a button-down shirt, not the College of Charleston T-shirt, but a real shirt with a collar. Claire hadn't asked him to wear it. He had chosen it himself, as he had been choosing many small things lately, trying to pay attention.

He carried a cake, not a gift card, but a cake from the bakery on Bay Street that had reopened under new management. Claire had watched him go in that morning and come out carrying a box. She didn't ask what was in it because Greg was really trying, and she wanted to let him try without trying to manage the outcome.

The cake was chocolate, Nina's favorite, not Claire's.

Greg had bought Nina's favorite cake for Nina's birthday party, which meant he had asked Claire what Nina liked, which meant he had paid attention to the answer.

And all of that meant more than the cake itself.

Claire found Nina in the kitchen and handed her the box.

"This is from Greg."

Nina opened it and looked at the chocolate cake.

"Greg bought me a cake?"

"Greg bought you a cake."

"Greg, who gave you the universal gift card, bought me a chocolate cake."

"He's a work in progress, what can I say?"

"Well, we're all works in progress," Nina said.

She put the cake on the counter next to Elena's flan.

Harper and Jordan arrived next.

Jordan's truck pulled into the crushed shell driveway, and Harper got out wearing linen instead of silk, which was an improvement so significant that Claire had texted Nina from across the yard.

She's wearing linen.

Nina texted back:

The end times are upon us.

Jordan got out of the driver's seat, carrying a bottle of wine and a small wrapped package. He wore jeans and a faded blue shirt.

He shook Greg's hand on the porch, and within three minutes, they were talking about the table Jordan was building, and Greg was asking about wood. Jordan was explaining the reclaimed church beams from Georgetown, and Claire watched her husband lean forward in his chair with genuine interest.

Sam arrived at noon.

He parked on the road because the driveway was full. He walked up the path to Nina's house carrying flowers for Nina and a separate, smaller bunch for Elena. He'd learned over the last few mont of very careful courtship that Elena was the gatekeeper, and the gatekeeper needed her own offering.

Elena accepted the flowers like a queen and then inspected the bouquet, smelling it. She looked at Sam over the top of the stems.

"You remembered I like gardenias," she said.

"You did mention it."

"I mentioned it once."

"I was listening."

Elena looked at him for a long moment and then nodded.

Sam found Nina in the kitchen. He kissed her on the cheek the way he did everything, gently.

"Happy birthday."

"Thank you for coming."

"Thank you for inviting me."

He looked around the kitchen. It was overflowing with food, and then there was the cake from Greg, the white napkins in a pile, and the napkin they'd all signed a year ago framed on the wall.

He'd heard the story of the pact. He'd heard all the stories over dinners and phone calls and long walks through his garden on James Island, but he'd never seen the napkin.

He walked over and looked at it.

"So this is it, the famous napkin."

"That's it."

"It's smaller than I imagined."

"The biggest things usually are."

He looked at her, and Nina thought about David looking at the marsh through that same kitchen window and saying, *this is it.*

She thought that maybe a person could have more than one *this is it* in a lifetime.

Maybe the first one didn't cancel out the second, and the second one didn't dishonor the first.

Maybe a life was big enough for two of them.

The party was everything a birthday dinner should be, loud and messy.

There were no place settings, no color-coordinated napkins, no Pinterest Mason jars. People sat where they wanted, ate what they wanted, and spilled things everywhere without any apology.

Greg talked to Jordan about wood grain for forty-five minutes and looked happier than Claire had seen him in years. It occurred to her that maybe she hadn't been paying close attention to him either.

Harper sat on the porch with a plate of empanadas and guarded them with her life. She did let Jordan rest his arm across the back of her chair, and she didn't stiffen or pull away.

Elena held court at the kitchen table, telling Sam stories about David as a child. They were either true or maybe slightly improved, but Sam listened with the patient attention of a man who understood that loving Nina now meant loving David's memory, and loving David's memory meant listening to Elena.

Listening to Elena, however, was an endurance sport that he had apparently trained for.

Lucia moved through the party like a stage

manager, refilling drinks and adjusting the music. She checked on the slideshow setup with intensity that she had inherited from her father.

She set up the laptop, connected it to the television in the living room, and at some point in the early afternoon, she stood on a chair and whistled.

The room went quiet.

"Attention," Lucia said. "I made something. I'm very proud of it. You're all going to watch it. Now, if you cry, there are napkins. They're white from the Piggly Wiggly. You're just going to have to deal with it."

She pressed play.

The slideshow opened with a photo from last year's birthday dinner. There were three women with their glasses raised, smiling.

This was the same photo they had looked at on Claire's living room floor the night before the skydive.

They were smiling, but something behind their eyes was not alive.

Lucia had set it to music.

The opening notes of "Man! I Feel Like a Woman!" filled the living room.

Claire laughed. Harper groaned and rolled her eyes, and Nina put her hand over her mouth.

The photos continued to play.

The stage at Hank's. Folly Beach at dawn. Their polka dot bathing suits, waist-deep in the December Atlantic.

There was a picture from Señora Morales's kitchen. Nina standing at the stove.

There was the rock-climbing wall, with Claire frozen halfway up. She wondered who had taken that photo.

There was the tattoo parlor and their wrists in a row.

Picture after picture after picture crossed the screen, bringing back memories that none of them would ever forget.

The final picture was at the skydive, the yellow plane, and the neon jumpsuits.

The last photo, which Lucia must have gotten from Cal because none of them had taken it, was of the three women on the field, holding each other, tiny against the enormous blue sky.

The song ended, and the room was quiet.

Elena was sobbing into a napkin, which she would totally deny later, of course.

Greg was holding Claire's hand, which he had reached for during the polar plunge photo and had never let go.

Jordan now had his arm fully around Harper, and Harper was leaning into him.

Sam stood behind Nina with his hand on her shoulder, and Nina covered his hand with hers.

Lucia finally stepped off the chair and looked at her mother.

"I know Dad would have made a spreadsheet," she said, "but I made a slideshow. It's still the same energy."

Nina pulled her daughter into a hug so tight that Lucia made a noise of protest. Elena got up from the table and put her arms around both of them.

These three generations of women who had loved David Vargas stood in the kitchen, holding each other, and everyone in the room went silent, allowing them that moment.

When the party wound down, they moved to the porch, Nina's porch, not Claire's this time. The tide was coming in, the water creeping over the mud, the egrets settling in for the night.

Claire sat in a rocking chair with Greg beside her, not across from her. He had pulled his chair closer without being asked, and their shoulders almost touched.

"This was a good party," Greg said.

"It was."

"No fancy napkins."

Claire rolled her eyes. "No fancy napkins."

"Better this way, I think."

Claire looked at him. He was looking out at the marsh, and it occurred to her that his face was softer than it used to be, or maybe it had always been soft, and she had just stopped looking closely enough to see it.

"Yeah, better this way."

Someone asked a question. Claire wasn't even sure who, maybe Harper or Nina, maybe Lucia.

"Are we doing it again? Are you doing it again? Year two?"

The three of them looked at each other, Claire, Harper, Nina, sitting on the porch, wine in hand, having just gotten through twelve scary adventures, or at least scary to them.

"We don't need a pact," Claire said.

"No, we don't," Harper agreed.

"That pact was just our training wheels," Nina said, "and we don't need training wheels anymore."

"But," Harper said.

"But," Claire said.

"We should probably still do things that scare us from time to time," Nina said, "just because."

"Just because," Harper agreed.

"Who's picking the first adventure?" Lucia's voice

came from inside the house, where she was eating leftover flan. "I am. I'm picking. You're all going to hate it so much."

"She can't pick," Harper said. "She didn't sign the napkin."

"The napkin has expired," Nina said. "New year, new rules."

"I want new rules," Lucia called. "Rule one, Abuela has to come."

Elena's voice came from the kitchen. "I am seventy-two years old, and I am not jumping out of an airplane."

"We're not asking you to jump out of an airplane, Elena," Nina said.

"Good, because I won't."

"We're just asking you to do one scary thing a month."

"Oh, nothing scares me. Well, I mean, except maybe the airplane thing."

"Abuela," Lucia said, "you screamed when you saw a lizard on your windshield last week."

"It was a very large lizard. I saw teeth. I swear it!"

The porch erupted in laughter.

Greg leaned over to Claire. "I want to come, too, to the next one, whatever it is."

Claire looked at her husband, at his face in the

porch light, older and kinder, at his hand on the arm of the rocking chair.

She reached for it.

"Okay," she said.

The porch light on Nina's house glowed warm against the Edisto dark. And inside, a framed napkin hung on the wall, faded and worn, bringing together the people who were already planning what came next.

The napkin now lived on Claire's wall, not the kitchen wall or the fridge where it had spent the first year, held up by a magnet, getting splashed by the dishwasher or bumped by grocery bags.

It had graduated.

Claire had taken it to a frame shop on Bay Street to get a proper frame, the same street where Nina's favorite bakery had reopened. A woman named Diane put it under glass in a simple white frame, handling it with care.

The frame hung in Claire's studio.

It was still technically the guest room. It still had a bed that was pushed against the wall to make room for her easel and supply table.

There were seven paintings hanging on the wall

now. The abstract from the class with its brave, messy colors; a watercolor of the Beaufort waterfront at sunrise; a small oil painting of their matching tattoos; a sketch of the view from the rock-climbing wall; and a painting of Hank's that she'd started from the photograph.

Two more were still in progress. One was the marsh at dawn, her version, different from Nina's. The other she hadn't named yet. It was just a painting of a porch light at night, three shapes in the chairs. It could have been any porch. It could have been every porch.

The room still smelled like turpentine and linseed oil.

The smell made Claire feel twenty years old and fifty-one at the same time, which was the best way to feel, rooted in who you've been, but present in who you are, and curious about who you'd be next.

It was Saturday morning in November, one month after the birthday party, two months after the skydive, and thirteen months since Harper had pulled out a pen and written on a napkin.

Claire stood in her studio, looking at the napkin on the wall.

She could hear Greg in the kitchen. He was making breakfast. He did this on Saturdays now, a routine that had started with the disastrous stir-fry, but had evolved with improvements and one small kitchen fire.

Now it was eggs, toast, and coffee, and the toast was only slightly too dark. The coffee was good, and the eggs were scrambled the way Claire liked them, because she had told Greg how she liked them, and he had remembered.

He remembered.

That was the new thing about Greg. He remembered things. Not all the time, and not perfectly. Sometimes he still forgot to take out the recycling, or he watched the Braves with more enthusiasm than he watched anything else. And sometimes he still retreated to the den on the evenings when the world felt like too much.

But he kept asking her questions.

He asked about the paintings, what her friends were up to, and who was coming over for dinner. He asked Claire about her day and actually waited for the answer.

They were not fixed. Claire didn't believe any marriage was ever fixed. She believed they were construction sites.

That was the metaphor she'd used at Dr. Warren's office.

Construction sites and marriages were messy,

loud, and full of things that might fall on your head, but they had a blueprint now, and they were both reading it.

Some days were good, and some days were hard.

Sometimes Greg said exactly the right thing, and sometimes he said exactly the wrong thing.

Sometimes they sat on the porch together and didn't say a word at all, but the silence was different than before.

It had space in it, room for two.

Claire turned from the napkin and looked around her studio.

The word still felt new in her mouth. A studio.

She'd spent twenty-seven years not painting. She'd spent twenty-six years making everything beautiful for everyone but herself.

And now she had this place that was just for her.

At 10 a.m., the doorbell rang.

Claire wasn't expecting anyone. Harper and Jordan were in Mount Pleasant for the weekend. Nina and Sam were on Edisto. Elena was at church, where she went every Saturday morning to light a candle for David and also argue with the priest about the temperature of the sanctuary.

Claire wiped her hands on her jeans, which were covered in paint.

A woman stood on the porch. She was young, maybe early 30s, with her dark hair pulled back. Her face looked like it had been crying a lot. She wore a cardigan even though it was warm this morning and wrapped it around herself like a shield. She held a casserole dish.

"Hi," the woman said. "I'm so sorry to bother you. My name is Jenna. I just moved in three houses down. I'm the, um…" She paused and took a breath. "I'm the one going through a divorce. I'm sure the neighbors have mentioned it. I know it's a small community."

"They haven't mentioned anything," Claire said, which was a lie because the women in her neighborhood had mentioned it to her at the grocery store, the post office, and the school parking lot. But Claire had decided years ago that other people's pain was not her gossip.

"I brought this," Jenna said, holding up the casserole. "I, I don't know, I guess to say hello. My mother always said to bring food when you move somewhere new. I think the tradition is actually supposed to go the other way, where the neighbors bring you food. But I just needed something to do with my hands."

Claire looked at the casserole dish and at Jenna, with her cardigan wrapped tight. She could tell she'd been crying. And she certainly understood hands that needed something to do.

She thought about how she was thirteen months ago, standing in this kitchen with flour under her fingernails and a gold wedding band and wondering, *Who am I?*

She thought about all of the adventures and all of the changes that she'd made.

It meant that someone had to go first at some point. Somebody had to say the honest thing.

"Come on in," Claire said. "My husband just made coffee. It's decent. He's getting better at it."

Jenna stepped inside. She set the casserole on the counter and looked around the kitchen. She could see the open door of the studio.

"What's that?" she asked, nodding.

"Which part?"

"There's something in a frame on the wall. Is that a napkin?"

"Oh." Claire smiled. She poured two cups of coffee. She handed one to Jenna and held the other, leaning against the kitchen counter. "It's a long story," Claire said. "Do you have time?"

Jenna wrapped her hands around the coffee mug and looked at Claire. "I've got nothing but time."

Claire took a sip of her coffee.

"Well, it all started with a birthday party," Claire said, "and a napkin color I just couldn't get right."

Jenna's head tilted to the side. "A napkin?"

"Yep. A napkin started it all."

The coffee cooled, and Claire told the story from the beginning to a woman who might have just needed it as much as she once did.

F ree Bonus Scene
Want to see where the women are five years later?

The birthday candles may be long gone, but these women still have plenty of life, laughter, friendship, and surprises ahead of them.

I wrote a special bonus scene just for readers of *Midlife Birthday Club*, where you can peek in on the women five years after the book ends and see what life looks like now.

Get it free here:

https://dl.bookfunnel.com/7ajpuuje6o

. . .

Read Next
If you enjoyed the friendship, fresh starts, and second chances in *Midlife Birthday Club*, I think you'll love my other books! Find all of my other books using my handy reading list!

https://store.rachelhannaauthor.com/pages/reading-order